I0748440

WISE Scholars Publishing
"We Bring LIFE to LEARNING"

First published by WISE Scholars Publishing, August 2015

Second Edition Published, July 2016

Atlanta, Georgia, USA

10 9 8 7 6 5 4 3 2 1

www.wisescholarspublishing.com

Library of Congress Cataloging-in-Publication Data

Wise, Frankie Berry

"Broken Promises"

Paperback

ISBN-10: 0996394656

ISBN-13: 978-0996394659

Hardback

ISBN-10: 0-9963946-6-4

ISBN-13: 978-0-9963946-6-6

Printed in the United States of America

DEDICATION

I dedicate this play to my beloved grandmother, Mrs. Lula Mae Bell Johnson Rutledge.

(December 7, 1890 – October 22, 1979)

ACKNOWLEDGEMENTS

Thank you to my longtime friend and dentist, Dr. N. Jeff Carden III, for editing *Broken Promises;* Christine L'Ecluse for helping to fine-tune the actions of its characters; Soweto Bosia for designing its impressive book cover; and WISE Scholars Publishing and my daughter, Marshalette Wise, for publishing several of my literary works.

A DRAMA IN FIVE ACTS

BROKEN PROMISES

Frankie Berry Wise

BROKEN PROMISES
CHARACTERS

SARAH JACKSON (a middle-aged mulatto woman) – **mother of Lilly, Rose, Cleo and John** (deceased); **grandmother of Iris**

LILLY JACKSON (a 21 year-old mulatto girl) – **oldest daughter of Sarah; mother of Iris**

ROSE JACKSON (a 17 year-old mulatto girl) – **daughter of Sarah; sister of Lilly, Cleo, and John**

CLEO JACKSON (a 25 or 30 year-old mulatto man) – **son of Sarah; brother of Lilly, Rose, and John**

IRIS JACKSON (age 8) (age 14) (adult) – **a mulatto girl; daughter of Lilly; granddaughter of Sarah**

SAMANTHA BOGGS (infant) (age 14) – **mulatto daughter of Iris**

SAMUEL BOGGS (an 18 year-old mulatto man) – **son of Henry and Emma; brother of Belinda; Iris' lover; father of Samantha**

BELINDA BOGGS (a 14 year-old mulatto girl) (adult) – **daughter of Henry and Emma; sister of Samuel**

MRS. EMMA BOGGS (a mulatto woman in her mid-thirties) – **wife of Henry; mother of Samuel and Belinda**

MR. HENRY BOGGS (a white man in his early forties) – **husband of Emma; father of Samuel and Belinda**

MR. PARKER JAMES (an elderly white man) – **employer of Sarah and the father of Rose, Lilly, Cleo, and John**

MRS. CORA MAE BUTLER (a middle-aged black woman) – **school teacher who owns and operates a school for colored girls; grandmother of Annie**

ANNIE BUTLER (age 10) (age 14) – **a dark skinned girl; granddaughter of Mrs. Cora Mae Butler**

MR CHARLIE SWEET (a 25 year-old white man) – **boarder at Sarah's house; Rose's lover**

MR. JOE FISH (a black man in his mid-twenties) – **boarder at Sarah's house; Iris' molester**

BOARDER ONE (a young black man) – **boarder at Sarah's house**

BOARDER TWO (a young black man) – **boarder at Sarah's house**

HATTIE SMITH (9 or 10 year-old black girl) (adult) – **twin sister of Mattie; classmate of Iris**

MATTIE SMITH (9 or 10 year-old black girl) (adult) – **twin sister of Hattie; classmate of Iris**

SEVEN EXTRA CLASSMATES (8, 9 or 10 year-old black girls) – **classmates of Iris**

MR. JACK JONES (a middle-aged black man) – **friend of the Jackson family**

MR. ABRAHAM GREEN (a middle-aged black man) – **husband of Mabel Green; adoptive father of Sarah**

MRS. MABEL GREEN (a middle-aged black woman) – **wife of Abraham Green; adoptive mother of Sarah**

BLACK SOLDIER (a young man)

WHITE SOLDIER (a young man)

MR. COOPER (a middle-aged white man) – **a mailman**

DOG (middle to older aged) – **a hound**

ACT I

SCENE 1

(SETTING: Iris is in the living room of her modest home. She is middle-aged and her hair is gray. She sits in Sarah's old rocking chair and clutches a white handkerchief, while rereading letters from the past that contain broken promises. There is a knock at the door.)

IRIS: (Loudly) "Who is it?"

MR. COOPER: (Loudly) "Mr. Cooper, your mailman."

IRIS: "Come on in, Mr. Cooper. The door is unlocked."

(Mr. Cooper enters the living room. He is dressed in a mailman's uniform - shirt and shorts - and carries a mailbag across his shoulder. He has mail in his hand, which he hands to Iris.)

MR. COOPER: "Here's your mail, Miss Iris."

(Iris takes the mail and quickly goes through it, before dropping it in a trash can next to her chair.)

IRIS: "That was kind of you, Mr. Cooper, but you could've left it in the mailbox. It's only junk mail."

MR. COOPER: "Miss Iris, I was beginning to worry about you; I haven't seen you in days. I used to see you just about every day. Either you're on the porch, swinging in the swing, or working in your flower or vegetable garden. Have you been sick?"

IRIS: "Thanks for being concerned, Mr. Cooper, but I'm alright. I haven't felt like doing anything since Lilly died. Now I sit here lonely, just reading old letters from the past. **(Iris shows Mr. Cooper each letter as she describes them.)** This one is the last letter I got from my Sam. He was killed in the war. **(Pause)** This letter is from my friend, Belinda. She would've been my sister-in-law if Sam and I had gotten married, but we didn't get the chance. **(Pause)** And this one, I received over a year ago from my and Sam's daughter, Samantha. She's my only child. I haven't seen her in years. **(Pause)** She didn't even come to Mama or Lilly's funeral. She's married to a white doctor and has twin daughters. She named them Sarah and Lilly, after my grandma and mama."

MR. COOPER: "That was thoughtful of her."

IRIS: "She sent me that picture of her, her husband, and the girls." **(Iris points to a framed picture of a white-looking family sitting on a table.)**

MR. COOPER: "That's a fine looking family."

IRIS: "Yes, it is. She said she and the girls were coming to visit me soon, but they haven't gotten here, yet. **(Pause)** I have this constant dream that Samantha and my granddaughters are standing over me while I'm sleeping in my bed. Samantha keeps calling me. She says, **(Iris calls out loudly as Mr. Cooper stands and listens patiently)** 'Mama! Mama! Wake-up', but when I do, I realize it's only a dream… I hope she'll keep her promise. **(Pause)** Mr. Cooper, do you have a wife and children?"

MR. COOPER: "My wife and I never had children. She died five years ago. I'm alone like you, so I know what loneliness feels like. **(Pause)** Miss Iris, you're the last person on my route. No one is waiting for me at home and if you would like to tell me your story, I'm a good listener."

IRIS: "Have a seat Mr. Cooper, **(Mr. Cooper sits in a chair and rests his mailbag against his hairy legs)** because this story is going to take a while. It starts in our old home right here in Cross Town, Georgia, in the winter of nineteen-forty…."

(The stage lights dim to black)

SCENE 2

(SETTING: The year is approximately 1940. This scene takes place in the bedroom of the Jackson's old home. There is a bed in each corner of the room, a small table with a kerosene lamp on top, and a dresser with a cracked mirror. On the wall hangs a framed photo of a young soldier. There is a fireplace where a fire once burned. In front of the fireplace sits a rocking chair. In one bed, under raggedy covers, Sarah and Rose are sleeping. In the other bed, Iris is sleeping alone because her mother, Lilly, is away. It is late at night and the bedroom is cold and lit only by the kerosene lamp.)

IRIS: (Whispers) "Aunt Rose! Aunt Rose! Aunt Rose!"

(There is a minute of silence before Rose finally speaks.)

ROSE: "What?"

IRIS: "I'm scared. I hear something in the hall."

ROSE: "It's only the wind." **(Pause)** Go back to sleep!"

IRIS: (Pleading) "Can I sleep with you and Mama?"

ROSE: "It's not enough room for three people."

IRIS: (Pleading) "Please sleep with me!"

ROSE: "It's too cold to get out of my bed and come over there. I'm right over here; besides, your bed smells like pee."

(Rose gets out of her bed and quietly goes over to Iris' bed. Iris feels a burst of cold air against her back. It is Rose, getting in bed with her.)

ROSE: (Whispers) "It's me. I'm scared of the dark, too. We sure could use a brave man around the house."

IRIS: "Uncle Cleo is brave. He's not afraid of the dark and old ghosts."

ROSE: "He spends most of his time in the woods, hunting and fishing."

IRIS: (Whispers) "Why?"

ROSE: "He's a hunter. He hunts animals for their meat and hides, and catches fish for us to eat. **(Pause)** Let's be quiet before we wake up Mama."

SARAH: "It's too late."

ROSE: "Sorry, Mama."

SARAH: (Angrily) "Never will I let a no good nigger, like George, live in my house, again!"

ROSE: (Whispers) "She's talking about your daddy. He used to live with us. Mama hates his guts."

IRIS: "I don't have a daddy."

ROSE: "Everybody has a daddy, silly."

IRIS: "No, I don't!"

ROSE: "Yes, you do!"

IRIS: "Where is he?"

ROSE: "I'll tell you tomorrow. **(Pause)** Now go to sleep!"

(The stage lights dim to black)

SCENE 3

(The next morning, Iris sits up in her bed. There is a fire burning in the fireplace. Sarah and Rose's bed is made. As usual, Sarah has left for her job at Mr. Parker James' store. Rose, wearing a long white cotton nightgown, is sitting in Sarah's rocking chair in front of the fireplace. When Iris - also wearing a long white cotton nightgown - sees Rose, she jumps out of bed and exits the stage.)

ROSE: "Close that door, before I freeze in here!"

(Iris returns a few seconds later.)

ROSE: "Did you pee on yourself?" **(Rose feels the hem of Iris' gown to see if it is wet.)**

IRIS: (Pushes Rose's hand away) "I made it in time."

(Iris sits on the floor in front of the fireplace. Beside the rocking chair, a large brown paper bag sits. Rose reaches for the bag and hands it to Iris.)

ROSE: "I thought you were never going to wake up."

(Iris takes the bag.)

ROSE: "It's from your mother, Lilly."

IRIS: "Aunt Rose… What's in it?"

ROSE: "I don't know! Look and see for yourself!"

(Iris looks inside the bag. She pulls out a blue dress, white socks, and underwear. At the bottom of the bag is a little white doll with blonde hair, dressed in a green corduroy dress. Rose observes as Iris ignores the hand-me-down clothing, leaving them lying on the floor, and begins to play with the doll.)

ROSE: "Why do they make white dolls pretty and black dolls ugly?"

IRIS: (Looks at Rose) "Are you white?"

ROSE: "Why you ask me that?"

IRIS: "You're the color of Miss Ann and you're pretty. Grandma, Mama, Uncle Cleo, and I look like you and we're pretty, too."

ROSE: (Smiling) "We just look white, but we're colored. We're caught in the middle. White women hate us because their husbands made us this color. The colored folks envy us because we can sometimes use our whiteness to our advantage. **(Pause)** As you get older, you'll see what I'm talking about." **(Pause)** "What're you going to name your doll?"

IRIS: "Miss Ann."

ROSE: "That's a good name for a white doll."

IRIS: "Aunt Rose… how did I get a daddy?"

ROSE: (Surprised that Iris had not forgotten the promise she made) "You don't need to know."

IRIS: "But, you promised."

ROSE: "I did. Didn't I? **(Pause)** If I do tell you, you must promise that you'll never tell Lilly or Cleo… and especially not Mama?"

IRIS: "I promise."

ROSE: "Cross your heart and hope to die?"

IRIS: (Crossing her heart) "Cross my heart and hope to die."

ROSE: (Getting comfortable in Sarah's rocking chair, begins to tell her story as Iris cuddles Miss Ann and listens.) "Your daddy's name was George Dawson. He came from Texas. He lived with us until Lilly got pregnant with you and then he just disappeared. That's the story." **(Rose gives Iris one of the two sweet potatoes from the ashes in the fireplace. Iris takes the sweet potato in her hand and without removing the skin begins to eat it quickly.)**

ROSE: "Don't eat that last sweet potato. It's for Mama. You sit here, keep warm by the fire, and play with Miss Ann." **(Rose stands)** "I'm going back to bed until Mama brings us our supper." **(Rose gets into her bed.)**

IRIS: "It's getting cold in here and I'm still hungry."

ROSE: "I'm not going in that cold kitchen to get more wood. Get in bed with me and wait for Mama. She'll be here soon."

(When Iris stands to get in bed with Rose, Sarah walks in the door. Sarah is a big, tall, very fair-skinned woman with long salt-and-pepper hair. Rose continues to lie in bed. Iris lays Miss Ann in the rocking chair. Sarah is carrying a platter of food covered with a dishtowel.)

SARAH: "I brought y'all some fried chicken, string beans, and corn muffins. **(Sarah looks at Rose lying in bed)** Rose, get out of that bed. I need you to help me spruce up the bedroom across the hall. A new white school is being built."

(Rose slowly gets out of bed and sits on its edge. Sarah exits the room.)

ROSE: "What's that got to do with us?" **(Loudly)** "WE can't go!"

(Sarah brings two plates of food into the bedroom. She gives one plate to Rose and the other to Iris, who has returned to her position on the floor with her doll. Sarah sits down in her rocking chair before she answers Rose.)

SARAH: "Mayor Berry came into the store today. He was looking for a good colored family to board three colored men that will be helping to build the new school. He asked Mr. Parker James if it was all right if they could board with us. Mr. James said it was all right with him.

We could use the extra money. I can pay for Iris to attend Cora Mae's School and go to college. **(Pause)** I want one of my children to amount to something. John ran off, joined the army, and was killed. Cleo is a wild man who lives with the wild animals. Lilly has a child and you are lazy to the bones. Maybe my grandbaby Iris will make me proud."

ROSE: "I thought you weren't going to let any more good-for-nothing, lowdown niggers stay with us again…even if Mr. James does own this house."

SARAH: (Giving Rose a sharp look) "This is different. This is business and you better watch your mouth, Miss Smarty-pants."

SARAH: (Looking at the doll on the floor next to Iris) "Where did this white doll come from?"

ROSE: (Chewing her food while she talks) "She was in that bag of hand-me-downs Lilly sent."

(Iris finishes eating. She gives the plate to Sarah and then takes Miss Ann off the floor and holds her.)

IRIS: "I named her Miss Ann."

SARAH: "That's a good name for a white doll."

(Rose gives Sarah her plate. Sarah takes the plates and exits the room,

leaving Iris sitting by the fireplace and Rose on the edge of her bed.)

ROSE: (Mumbling) "It's going to be like the last time when Mr. James insisted that no good, lowdown, George Dawson live with us. He became Mama's man and your daddy. If one of those new niggers puts a hand on me, I'm going to cut his wiener off."

(Rose looks at a confused Iris. She goes and sits in Sarah's rocking chair and tries to explain.)

ROSE: "It wasn't your mama's fault. Lilly was just a child and didn't know better. It was Mama's fault for leaving us home alone with that nigger. Just as soon as Mama left for work, George would make Cleo take the shotgun and go shoot squirrels for supper. He would send me under the house to search for doodlebugs. Lilly couldn't go with me. George said she had to wash the breakfast dishes. **(Pause)** The dishes were still dirty when he called me back in the house. So I got wise. **(Pause)** One day, I slipped back in the house. I didn't see George or Lilly, but I heard noises coming from his room. I went and peeped through the missing doorknob hole. Nine months later you were born."

(Rose and Iris stare into the fireplace at the dying flames. Finally, Iris looks at Rose.)

IRIS: "Aunt Rose, what's a doodlebug?"

ROSE: (Laughing) "I'll tell you later."

(Sarah enters the room. She is carrying extra logs and places them in the fireplace.)

SARAH: "What are you two giggling about?"

ROSE: "Nothing, Mama."

SARAH: "Iris, you and Miss Ann go to bed. Rose and I will be going across the hall to get the room ready for those boarders."

(Iris takes Miss Ann and goes to get into her bed, but Sarah stops her.)

SARAH: "You forgot to say your prayers!"

(Iris kneels beside her bed as Sarah and Rose wait impatiently.)

IRIS: "God bless my Mama Sarah, my Mama Lilly, my Aunt Rose, and my Uncle Cleo." **(She starts to get into bed, but again stops.)** And bless Miss Ann. **(Iris gets into bed.)**

(The room goes dark.)

ROSE: "Good night,
Sleep tight,
Don't let the bedbugs bite.
Soon it will be light,

They only come out at night."

SARAH: "Shut-up Rose!"

ROSE: "Yes, Mama."

(The stage lights dim to black)

SCENE 4

(Three colored men: Mr. Joe Fish, Man One, and Man Two are sitting at the Jackson's kitchen table. They are eating supper. As usual—every Friday after supper, Man One and Man Two go home for the weekend. Mr. Fish does not; He remains at the Jackson house. Man One and Man Two get up from the table.)

MAN ONE: "Miss Jackson, that meal was so delicious. If I wasn't married, I would ask for your hand."

MAN TWO: (Nodding in agreement) "I wish my wife could cook like you." **(Turning to Man One)** "Will you give me a ride downtown? I don't want to miss catching that bus home. My old lady is waiting for my paycheck."

MAN ONE: "My wife and children are waiting for mine. We better get going."

MAN TWO: (Looking at Mr. Fish, who remains sitting at the table) "Joe, do you need us to give you a ride somewhere?"

MR. JOE FISH: (He smiles as he looks over at Sarah, who is standing near the kitchen stove. She smiles back.) I'm going to hang around here for the weekend. See what's going on with the fine ladies of Cross Town. Just may find me a good woman to marry, like you two did."

MAN ONE: (Chuckling) "If you're talking about the likes of Miss Wilma Lee, you'll catch more than a wife." **(Man One and Man Two give Mr. Fish a sly look as they exit the kitchen.)**

SARAH: "Rose... you and Iris come in here! **(Rose and Iris enter. Sarah gives Rose a small brown paper sack of teacakes.)** You and Iris go out back and sit under the chinaberry tree and eat your teacakes. Mr. Fish and I are going to talk while I clean the kitchen."

ROSE: (Rose takes the bag) "Come on, Iris. It's time for me to show you what a doodlebug is." **(Rose and Iris exit the kitchen.)**

(The stage lights dim to black)

SCENE 5

(Rose and Iris are sitting in a swing on the porch. Rose has a school reader [book] and pencil in her hand. Iris is combing Miss Ann's hair. Rose hands Iris the book. Iris takes the book and throws it on the floor. Rose retrieves the book and tries to give it back to Iris, but she refuses to take it.)

ROSE: "Mama wants you to go over your lesson. Take this tablet and stop playing with that doll!"

IRIS: (Iris takes the book, but continues to hold Miss Ann.) "Her name is Miss Ann. I like playing with Miss Ann."

ROSE: "One day, you'll have a real baby of your own."

IRIS: "I don't want a real baby."

ROSE: "Iris, stop acting silly and recite your times tables to me."

IRIS: "I know my times table. Why do I have to keep repeating them?"

ROSE: "So you won't be behind the other girls when you start Mrs. Cora Mae's school."

IRIS: "I don't want to go to Mrs. Cora Mae's school! You can be my teacher."

ROSE: "You're already eight years old. You need to know more than I can teach you. Mama wants you to go to college. Mrs. Cora Mae's School for Colored Girls will give you that chance. If you're very smart, you can be in college by the time you're fifteen… maybe even at fourteen."

IRIS: "But I always hear Mama calling Mrs. Cora Mae a bitch."

ROSE: Maybe Mama does… but, don't let her hear you saying that word. Besides, what's between Mama and Mrs. Cora Mae has nothing to do with you. **(Rose slaps at insects flying around her head.)** These mosquitoes are eating me alive and it's hot out here! **(She scratches at mosquito bites on her arms and legs.)** Let's go inside!"

IRIS: "I don't want to go inside. I want to sit here and wait for Mama."

ROSE: (Getting up to leave) "Stay out here if you want to! I don't care if the mosquitoes drink all of your blood and the sun turns you black. But, you better not leave this swing. **(Pause)** I'm going inside to get a nap. I'll be back out here before Mama gets off work. Mama would kill me if she finds out I left you out here by yourself. **(Leaving to go inside, Rose pauses)** Iris, did you hear me?"

IRIS: (Continuing to comb Miss Ann's hair) "I heard you! I'll be sitting right here when you wake up."

(Rose exits the porch. A few moments pass before Mr. Fish appears.)

MR. JOE FISH: "Hello, Iris. **(Iris does not look up nor respond to Mr. Fish. She continues to comb Miss Ann's hair.)** You're playing with your doll?"

IRIS: "Yes, sir."

MR. JOE FISH: (Looking to see if anyone else is close by) "Where's Rose?"

IRIS: "In the house sleeping."

MR. JOE FISH: "Where's your Mama?"

IRIS: "At work."

MR. JOE FISH: "You're out here all by yourself?"

IRIS: "Yes, sir."

(Mr. Fish sits in in the swing with Iris. She quickly moves over to keep space between them.)

MR. JOE FISH: "Does your doll have a name?"

IRIS: "Miss Ann."

MR. JOE FISH: "Miss Ann! That's a good name for a white doll. **(Pause)** Iris, do you want to go in the house with me? I got some pennies in my room. You can have them to buy candy… But, we got to be quiet. We don't want to wake up Rose."

IRIS: "Aunt Rose told me not to leave the porch."

MR. JOE FISH: (Taking Iris by her hand) "Come on. We'll be back before Rose wakes up. You can bring your doll with you."

(Iris and Mr. Fish go inside the house. A short time elapses before she is forcefully pushed, without Miss Ann, back onto the porch by Mr. Fish. She again sits in the swing, wishing she had listened to Rose. A few moments later, Mr. Fish returns. He has a pillowcase filled with his clothes flung across his shoulder. He is in a hurry to leave, but hesitates.)

MR. JOE FISH: "Iris is you going to tell your grandma about what I did to you?"

IRIS: "No, sir."

MR. JOE FISH: "Good girl. As long as you keep our secret, nothing bad will happen to you." **(Mr. Fish hurriedly exits the stage.)**

ROSE: (Rushing back on the porch and sitting next to Iris) "Thank goodness, I woke up before Mama got home! **(Observing tears in Iris' eyes and her disheveled dress)** Are you crying?"

IRIS: (Drying her tears with her hand) "I'm not crying."

ROSE: "Yes, you are. I'm looking right at you. Did something happen while I was asleep? Where is Miss Ann?"

IRIS: "I left her in Mr. Fish's room."

ROSE: "Mr. Fish's room! Why were you in Mr. Fish's room? What did he do to you?"

IRIS: "Nothing." **(Sobbing)**

ROSE: "Did he touch you?"

IRIS: (looking down with embarrassment)

ROSE: (frantically) "Oh my God! Why did I leave you alone? **(Begging)** Iris, please don't tell Mama I left you alone or that you were in Mr. Fish's room. **(Pause)** He'll be gone by the first of next month, anyway. You won't ever see him again. Later, I'll help you look for Miss Ann."

IRIS: "I don't want Miss Ann anymore."

ROSE: "Okay! But, don't say anything to Mama about what happened today?"

IRIS: (In a sad voice) "I won't."

ROSE: "Good girl. Mama would kill me if she knew. Here she comes now!"

SARAH: (Walking on the porch and sitting between Rose and Iris.) "Rose, have you seen Mr. Fish today?"

ROSE: (Giving Iris a pleading look) "No ma'am."

SARAH: "Have you Iris?"

IRIS: "No, ma'am."

SARAH: "My friend, Wade, just left Mr. James' store. He said he saw Joe Fish stealing a ride on a boxcar. He said Joe had a pillowcase filled with something thrown across his shoulder. I bet that son-of-bitch, no-good nigger took my pillow case, filled it with his clothes, and skipped town without paying me my rent money!" **(Sarah pauses and stares at Iris.)** Why are you looking so sad? I bet I know. You're worried about starting school tomorrow."

IRIS: "Yes, ma'am."

SARAH: "I have a surprise for you. Those white folks gave Lilly the day off. She'll be here early in the morning to walk you to school. **(Sarah hugs Iris)** You feel better now?"

IRIS: "Yes, ma'am."

SARAH: "Girls, come with me to Fish's room. I want to see if his stuff is gone."

IRIS: (Resisting) "I don't want to go!"

SARAH: "Then stay here with Rose and I'll go." **(Sarah leaves.)**

ROSE: (Whispering) "Iris, what did Mr. Fish do to you when you were in his room?"

IRIS: "He gave me some grape Kool-Aid and laid me on his bed."

ROSE: (Checking to see if Sara was returning) "What else did he do?"

IRIS: "He took my panties off and laid on top of me. I remembered you told me what my daddy did to Lilly when she got me. I don't want to have a baby. I told him I was going to tell Mama."

ROSE: "And what did he do?"

IRIS: "He got off me and told me to put my panties back on. He told me to go and sit in the swing and not tell you or Mama. He said if I did, he'd kill all of us."

ROSE: "Don't worry Iris. You're too young to have a baby. You'll be alright. I'll help you look for Miss Ann later."

IRIS: "I don't ever want to see that ugly doll again!"

SARAH: (Returning) "Joe Fish is gone! His closet and dresser-drawers are empty. **(Very loudly and angrily)** May he burn in Hell!"

(The stage lights dim to black)

ACT II

SCENE 1

(In Mrs. Cora Mae's one room school, there are eight or nine schoolgirls sitting quietly in their chairs gazing at Lilly and Iris, who sit in a corner. They are patiently waiting for Mrs. Cora Mae's undivided attention. Mrs. Cora Mae sits at her desk as she leafs through papers that are scattered atop of it. Iris tightly holds Lilly's hand, who is frightened to be in the company of so many girls that are strangers.)

IRIS: (Whispering) "I want to go home… please!"

LILLY: (Whispering) "Iris, you got to stay here and be taught properly by Mrs. Cora Mae."

IRIS: "Aunt Rose can teach me."

LILLY: "That lazy sister of mine doesn't have the qualifications that Mrs. Cora Mae has. Mrs. Cora graduated from a college up north. **(Pause)** I think she did. At least that's what she's been telling everyone from the first day she moved to Cross Town. That's why she started this school. Mrs. Cora wants colored girls to have a better education and more choices than marrying young, having a bunch of stupid children or working as a maid for white people, like I do… nursing their children for a little money, breaking their backs picking cotton in fields owned by white people, or living the rest of their lives in this redneck Cross Town, Georgia. **(Pause)** Mama and I work hard to pay a woman that we both hate, so you can have the opportunity to become somebody. So you don't be like me, who's been working for white people since I was thirteen or like Mama, a slave to Mr. James, or your Aunt Rose, whose only hope is to use her beauty by passing for white to marry a rich white man."

MRS. CORA MAE: "Children, open your readers and go over your lesson. I will be with you in a minute. But, first I want to introduce you to Miss Lilly and her daughter, Iris. Stand up, Miss Lilly. **(Lilly stands)** Girls, this is Miss Lilly. Say 'hello' to Miss Lilly."

GIRLS: "Hello, Miss Lilly."

MRS. CORA MAE: "And stand up, Iris. **(Iris stands)** This is her daughter, Iris, your new classmate. **(Pause)** "Say 'hello' to Iris."

GIRLS: "Hello, Iris."

MRS. CORA MAE: "Lilly, it would be best for Iris if you leave now."

LILLY: "I promised her I would stay with her until I have to go back to my job."

MRS. CORA MAE: "Lilly, it's the rule. If you want Iris to be taught by me, you must obey the rules."

LILLY: "Yes, ma'am. **(Lilly looks at Iris)** Iris, I got to leave. Rose will be here after school to walk you home." **(As Lilly exits the stage, she slightly turns and waves goodbye to Iris, who waves back.)**

MRS. CORA MAE: (Taking Iris by the shoulders) "Iris, let me show you to your seat. **(Mrs. Cora Mae takes Iris to her seat, next to Annie.)** You'll be sitting next to my granddaughter, Annie."

(Annie is a very dark-complexioned girl, who looks and dresses like a boy.)

MRS. CORA MAE: "You and Annie can be friends."

(Iris sits in her seat, but she and Annie do not acknowledge each other.)

MRS: CORA MAE: "Girls, I have to run down to my house. I left some notes that I need. It won't take long. In the mean time, you girls can mingle and get acquainted with Iris."

GIRLS: "Yes, ma'am."

(Mrs. Cora Mae leaves the classroom. Mattie goes to talk to Iris. Hattie, Mattie's twin sister, follows her.)

MATTIE: "Hi Iris. My name is Mattie. This is my twin sister, Hattie."

HATTIE: "Are you white?"

IRIS: "NO!"

MATTIE: "I bet you think you're something just because you look white."

ANNIE: "Leave her alone you yellow bitches."

(All of the girls laugh out loud.)

MATTIE: "Sorry, Annie! I didn't mean to be rude to your GIRLFRIEND!"

(Mattie and Hattie return to their seats. They and the other girls begin chanting.)

"Annie is a boy. Annie is a boy.

Why? My mama said so.

Annie is a boy. Annie is a boy.

My mama ought to know.

When she was on the way,

My mama helped that day.

Annie is a boy. Annie is a boy."

HATTIE: "We don't want to be friends with either of you freaks!"

MATTIE: "Do we, girls?"

GIRLS: (In unison) "No."

HATTIE: (Hands on her hips) "Don't either of you come around us at recess time, either!"

ANNIE: "We can be best friends. We don't need them. If it's all right with your mama, maybe you could come to my house to play. Maybe you can stay overnight. We can catch lightning bugs and put them in a jar. We can turn them loose in my bedroom when the light is off."

IRIS: **(Shrugs her shoulders)** "Maybe."

(The stage lights dim to black)

SCENE 2

(It is three years later. Iris is at Mrs. Cora Mae and Annie's house. Iris is now eleven-years old and Annie is thirteen-years old. They are in Annie's bedroom, which is lit by a kerosene lamp. Iris and Annie are dressed for bed and are sitting on the edge of Annie's bed. They are gossiping about their hopes and dreams for the future after they have graduated from Mrs. Cora Mae's school.)

IRIS: "I'm glad my grandmother let me stay overnight at your house. I'm also glad she made me go to your grandmother's school three years ago. If I hadn't, I wouldn't have you as my best friend or be going to college. **(Iris looks at Annie.)** Annie, let's go to the same college. You're just as smart as I am. We both can become teachers and make our parents proud. We can return to Cross Town, Georgia and start a school where colored girls and boys can come and learn. **(Iris crosses her arms across her chest)** Then I want to get married to a dark colored man and have lots of pretty dark-skinned children… that are dark just like you Annie."

ANNIE: "Iris, I hope your dreams come true. But, your dreams are not mine. I don't want to go to college. I don't want be a teacher or marry a dark colored man and have a bunch of dark colored children. Once I leave, I don't ever want to come back to Cross Town. I hate this place and the people in it. I hate the colored people more than I do the white people. All colored people do is gossip. They say the day I was born, my mama was only able to hold me for a few minutes before she died. **(Showing anger)** If I could, I would leave Cross Town, Georgia tonight!"

IRIS: "If you left Cross Town, where would you go?"

ANNIE: "I'd catch a train to Detroit."

IRIS: "Who would you live with?"

ANNIE: "I'd live with my Aunt Evelyn and get a job in one of those factories that she's always talking about. She worked in one and made a lot of money. Now she owns a beauty parlor. When I make a lot of money, I'll get my own apartment and open my own beauty shop, too. Once I leave from here, I'll NEVER, EVER return to Cross Town, Georgia or the South again!"

MRS. CORA MAE: (Wearing her nightgown, enters Annie's bedroom) "You girls go to sleep. Tomorrow is a school day. My room is across the hall and I don't want to hear any talking or giggling."

ANNIE: "Yes, ma'am."

MRS. CORA MAE: "Iris that goes for you, too."

IRIS: "Yes, ma'am."

MRS. CORA MAE: (Taking the lamp and leaving) "Goodnight."

(The room goes dark.)

ANNIE: "Let's play a game."

IRIS: (Loudly) "What kind of game?"

ANNIE: "Quiet! Grandma will hear you. Let's pull the covers over our heads."

IRIS: "Okay" **(After some movements under the covers)** "Stop, Annie! I don't like playing this game. I'm going to tell my mama."

ANNIE: "I won't do it again. Please don't tell!"

IRIS: "Well. Okay, but don't do it again! And don't you tell either."

ANNIE: "I promise."

(The stage lights dim to black)

SCENE 3

(The next morning, Iris awakens to find Annie out of bed. She can hear Mrs. Cora Mae and Annie talking in the kitchen. Iris sits up and listens. In a tearful voice, Annie lies to her grandmother about what happened, last night, as she slept with Iris.)

ANNIE: "…and I told her I didn't want to be her friend anymore!"

MRS. CORA MAE: "That heifer! I should have known that I couldn't trust anyone related to Sarah Jackson. Don't you worry baby. I'll protect you from that little slut. Shame on Iris! I ought to tell her grandmother Sarah… but she's a slut, too. She's the reason your granddaddy left me."

ANNIE: "I don't ever want to see Iris again! Can I go and live with Aunt Evelyn? I can work in her beauty parlor. She can teach me how to be a beautician. Aunt Evelyn said I was welcome to come and live with her any time I wanted to. **(Begging)** Please, Grandma. Can I go and live with Aunt Evelyn?"

MRS. CORA MAE: "What about finishing your last year in school? Don't you want to go to college?

ANNIE: "No, ma'am."

MRS. CORA MAE: "Baby, are you sure? I have big plans for you."

ANNIE: "I'm sure, Grandma!"

MRS. CORA MAE: "Okay… if that's what you want to do…I'll see how soon I can get you on a train. **(Pause)** But if you ever change your mind… you can always come back home."

ANNIE: "Thank you, Grandma!" **(Giving her grandmother a hug).**

MRS. CORA MAE: "Annie, you go to my room. I want to talk to Iris alone."

ANNIE: "Yes, ma'am. **(After Annie quickly exits the stage, Mrs. Cora Mae calls Iris into the kitchen.)**

MRS. CORA MAE: (Loudly) "Iris!" **(Pause)** "Iris!"

IRIS: (Loudly) "Yes, ma'am."

MRS. CORA MAE: (Loudly) "Are you dressed?"

IRIS: (Softly) "No, ma'am."

MRS. CORA MAE: (Loudly) "Get dressed, so you can eat your breakfast."

IRIS: (Softly) "I'm not hungry. Can I stay in the room until we leave for school?"

MRS. CORA MAE: (Loudly) "No! Come and eat you breakfast, NOW!"

(Iris enters the kitchen and sits at the table. She does not make eye contact with Mrs. Cora Mae, who carelessly slops some food on a plate before handing it to her. Mrs. Cora Mae then sits next to Iris.)

MRS. CORA MAE: (Tugging on Iris' shoulder) "Iris! Raise your head and eat your breakfast!"

IRIS: (Looking down at the plate of food that looks like pig slop) "I'm not hungry."

MRS. CORA MAE: "Iris, Annie told me what you tried to do to her last night. The Bible says that people like you are not welcome in Heaven. But, I'm going to pray for you anyway and if you repent your sin, God may forgive you."

IRIS: (Looking directly at Mrs. Cora Mae) "People like me? What about people like you and Annie? Is God going to forgive her for lying on me? Is God going to forgive you for knowing the truth, but pretending you don't?"

MRS. CORA MAE: "Don't sass me young lady! You sit right here until I get dressed. I'm closing the school for today so I can help Annie pack her suitcase. She's going to Detroit to live with her Aunt Evelyn. Now that Annie is leaving… that white-looking girl, Belinda Boggs, can have her seat in school. You two should be birds of the same feather! **(Pause)** And, let me tell you this, missy… if you want to continue attending my school, don't tell Sarah what happened between you and Annie. You just tell Sarah that I had some important business to tend to downtown and I'll see you back at school tomorrow. You hear me?"

IRIS: "Yes, ma'am. I won't tell."

(Mrs. Cora Mae exits the stage and Annie immediately enters.)

IRIS: "Annie, why did you lie on me about last night? I wasn't going to tell anyone. I still want us to be best friends. If you leave, I'll be all alone. Please don't go."

ANNIE: "Iris, we can't be friends anymore. I don't ever want to see you again!

IRIS: "I'll always love you, Annie. You'll always be my best friend."

ANNIE: (Looking down embarrassed and sad) "I love you too… But, your love for me is different than mine."

MRS. CORA MAE: (From another room) "Come on, Iris. I'm ready to go!"

(Iris gets up from the table to leave. She tries to hug Annie, but Annie

refuses.)

IRIS: (As she exits the kitchen) "Goodbye, Annie. I'm glad you got your wish!"

(Annie sits down at the kitchen table with her head bowed. Iris exits the stage.)

(The stage lights dim to black)

SCENE 4

(It is later that same day. When Iris gets home, it is quiet inside the house. Iris checks to see if Rose is asleep in their bedroom. She hears Mr. Charlie Sweet and Rose's voices coming from Mr. Sweet's bedroom. Mr. Charlie Sweet is Sarah's, one and only, white boarder. Iris opens Mr. Sweet's bedroom door to find Rose and him in bed together. Iris stares at them until Rose and Charlie notice her. Mr. Charlie Sweet jumps up and then grabs his clothes and shoes off the floor, shielding himself with them, and leaves the room. Rose, wearing a white slip, pulls the covers up around her shoulders and sits up in bed.)

ROSE: (Upset) "Why are you home? You should be at school!"

IRIS: "Mrs. Cora Mae had to close the school for today. She had some business to take care of downtown. **(Pause)** I saw what y'all were doing."

ROSE: "Oh, we weren't doing anything but talking… that's all."

IRIS: "You think I don't know what's going on between you and Mr. Charlie Sweet… but I see how you two look at each other. And, I see how he takes more than one bath a week, coming home early and leaving late… always giving you a rose from Mama's flower garden or bringing you a candy bar from Mr. James' store. I see how you put on lipstick and wipe it off when you think it's time for Mama to come home. If Mama finds out that Mr. Charlie is romancing you, she will kill him!"

ROSE: "I know! So please don't tell her before we do! Charlie and I are planning to tell her tonight that he and I are…"

SARAH: (Entering Mr. Charlie Sweet's bedroom, she finds Rose in his bed.) "Rose! Why are you in Charlie's bed? **(Sarah pulls back the bed covers, exposing Rose in her slip. Rose tries to shield herself.)** You better have a good reason for shaming me or I'm going to whip you! **(Pause)** With my bare hands, I'm going to kill Charlie Sweet!"

ROSE: (Pulling the covers back around her shoulders) "Charlie! Charlie! Mama's home! We better talk to her NOW."

(Mr. Charlie Sweet returns to the bedroom fully dressed.)

ROSE: "Tell her, Charlie!"

MR. CHARLIE SWEET: "Baby, you better tell her."

SARAH: (Hands on her wide hips) "SOMEBODY had better start talking!"

MR. CHARLIE SWEET: "Miss Sarah, Rose and I are in love. We're getting married. We hope you'll give us your blessing."

(Without responding, Sarah grabs Mr. Charlie Sweet by the collar of

his shirt. She pins him against the wall and begins to choke the small statured man. Rose jumps out of bed and tries to intervene between Sarah and Charlie.)

ROSE: (Screaming) "Mama, please don't kill Charlie! I love him!" **(Rose pulls Sarah away from Charlie and then stands between them. Charlie's back is against the wall.)**

SARAH: "Charlie Sweet, you white trash, stop hiding behind a woman!"

MR. CHARLIE SWEET: (Standing behind Rose) "I'm sorry, Miss Jackson. I didn't mean for you to find out about Rose and me this way. I love Rose. You got to believe me!"

SARAH: "Now I know why I couldn't find you to help me lift Mr. James in his bed. You were here messing with my Rose!"

ROSE: "I'm sorry, Mama!"

SARAH: (Looking at Rose and talking in a calmer voice) "My baby girl, my sweet Rose…how could you lay with the likes of Charlie Sweet?"

ROSE: (Nervously) "Charlie and I love each other, Mama. I'm going to have his baby. We didn't mean for it to happen, but it did. Please

Mama, you of all people should understand. I love him the same way you love Mr. Parker James."

SARAH: "I don't love that old, white Parker James. I hate him. I'm looking forward to the day I see him dead! I don't want the same thing to happen to you. Please listen to me."

ROSE: "But, Mama, I love Charlie! **(In tears)** "I love him!"

MR. CHARLIE SWEET: (Coming from behind Rose and gently hugging and consoling her) "I love Rose, too, Miss Jackson. You got to believe me!"

SARAH: (Staring at them for a few seconds before sitting in a chair; in a tired voice) "Charlie Sweet, I'm not going to kill you, but I want you to leave my house right now and never come back."

MR. CHARLIE SWEET: (Rose and Charlie look at each other determining who will speak.) "Miss Sarah, I'll leave your house, but Rose is coming with me."

SARAH: (Standing up) "The HELL she is!"

(Rose takes a small suitcase from behind the bed. She is crying and wiping her tears with a white, lace handkerchief. She quickly picks up a dress from the floor and puts it on. She then puts on a pair of

shoes.)

ROSE: "Mama, my bag is packed. I was going to tell you tomorrow. I guess today is just as good. When Charlie goes, I'm going with him."

SARAH: "If you disobey me and go away with that white trash, you'll be *breaking the chain* with this family. **(Pointing her finger at Mr. Sweet)** If you leave, don't you EVER, EVER, come back!"

ROSE: (In a disbelieving voice) "Not ever, Mama?"

SARAH: (In a high pitched voice) "Not EVER!"

ROSE: (Turning to Iris, who looks on in disbelief) "Iris, please take care of yourself and Mama."

IRIS: "Aunt Rose, please don't go. Mama and I love you."

ROSE: (Looking at Iris sympathetically) "I love you and Mama, too… but, I also love Charlie. **(Pause)** One day, you'll understand when you fall in love. **(Taking Iris by the hand)** Tell Cleo and Lilly that I love them… and no matter what Mama says, I promise I'll see y'all again."

MR. CHARLIE SWEET: (Picking up the suitcase from the floor and grabbing Rose's hand. Rose then let's go of Iris' hand.) "Miss Jackson, I will love and care for Rose and your grandchild for the rest of my life."

ROSE: "I guess this is goodbye. I love you, Mama." **(Mr. Charlie Sweet and Rose quickly exit the stage.)**

SARAH: (Hurrying to the door and calling out to Rose in a defeated voice) "I'm sorry, Rose! I didn't mean what I said. I'll help you raise your baby. Please come back!" **(A few seconds pass before a tearful Sarah turns to Iris.)** Will she take care of herself? Will we see her again?"

IRIS: (Comforting Sarah) "She will Mama… and we'll see her again."

SARAH: "But when?"

(The stage lights dim to black)

ACT III

SCENE 1

(It is now four years later. Lilly has moved back home from where she was working as a live-in maid to work fulltime for her brother, Cleo. She is managing his café, *Cleo's Place.* Sarah, Lilly, and Cleo are sitting at the kitchen table. Sarah is sorting a basket of dirty clothes to be washed. Lilly is putting on her shoes. Cleo is drinking a cup of coffee while he waits to drive Lilly to the café. Iris is in the bedroom asleep.)

SARAH: (Shouting from the kitchen) "Iris, get out of bed and get dressed! I need you to clean the house while I wash the clothes."

(Iris enters the kitchen. She is wearing one of Lilly's housedresses. Her hair is uncombed and she is barefooted.)

SARAH: "Sleepyhead, did you and Belinda Boggs have a good time at the class dance?"

IRIS: "It was alright."

LILLY: "Iris, tell Mama about SAMUEL."

SARAH: "Who is SAMUEL?"

LILLY: "Don't be shy. Tell Mama about Samuel, Belinda's brother."

SARAH: "She's not going to tell me, Lilly, so you go on and tell me."

LILLY: "Okay. We were late going to get Iris from the dance, so Sam and Belinda drove her back to the café in his car. Cleo was locking the door when this car suddenly drove up with Iris and Belinda. Iris was in the front seat and Belinda Boggs was in the back. Only Iris and this strange boy got out of the car. I thought he was white. I said, 'Iris, why are you home so early and who is this boy you're with?'"

CLEO: "Lilly was fixing to scream at the poor boy. I told her to give the boy a chance to explain. So Lilly and I sat on the steps to hear what he had to say. He said he was Samuel Boggs. Lilly and I thought he was white until he said he was Belinda's brother. I told him the only other Boggs I know was old redneck, Jim Boggs. I was so embarrassed when he told me Mr. Jim was his uncle. He said his daddy was Jim's younger brother. I apologized. Then he said it was getting late and he had to get his sister home. He wished us goodnight and he left. I thought he was a nice fellow. Didn't you, Iris?"

SARAH: "Cleo, you and Lilly go to work and stop teasing Iris."

(Cleo sets his empty coffee cup on the table. He and Lilly are leaving as Samuel Boggs is waiting at the door.)

CLEO: "Sam! Why are you here?"

SAMUEL: "I'm here to see Iris…If you don't mind."

LILLY: "That's left up to Mama."

(Sam enters the kitchen. Iris looks ashamed of her appearance.)

SARAH: "Who are you, boy?"

SAMUEL: "I'm Samuel Boggs, Belinda's brother. You can call me Sam."

SARAH: "Sam, why are you here?"

SAMUEL: "Miss Jackson, can I come and court Iris?"

SARAH: (shocked) "You don't waste time. Do you boy?"

SAMUEL: "No, ma'am."

SARAH: "How old are you, Sam?"

SAMUEL: "Eighteen."

SARAH: "Three years older than Iris. Iris, do you want to court Sam? **(Pause)** Well, speak up! Do you or don't you?"

IRIS: (Looking down at the floor) "I don't mind."

SARAH: "You can visit Iris on Sunday evenings, but you can only stay for an hour."

SAMUEL: "Maybe one Sunday, you'll let me take her to my house to meet my mama and daddy?"

SARAH: "You better be glad I agreed to let you come to our house. I don't know you or your parents that well! Iris can't leave this house alone with you until I get to know you better. If you and Iris are still friends after three months, then maybe you can take her to visit your parents."

SAMUEL: "I'll be looking forward to that day. Iris I'll see you next Sunday evening."

SARAH: (Looking at Iris) "Is that alright with you, Iris?"

IRIS: "Yes, ma'am."

SAMUEL: "Good day, Miss Sarah." **(Sam exits the stage.)**

(The stage lights dim to black)

SCENE 2

(It is three months later. The setting is the home of Mr. Henry and Mrs. Emma Boggs, the parents of Samuel and Belinda. Mr. Henry, Mrs. Emma, and Belinda are in the kitchen. Belinda is setting the table with their best dishes. Mrs. Emma fills bowls and platters, from pots of food on the stove, and sets them on the table. Mr. Henry is seated at the table. He is dressed in tobacco-stained overalls, a plaid shirt, and work boots. Dog, a hound, lies under the table. Mrs. Emma wants everything perfect because Sam is bringing his girlfriend, Iris, to dinner. Sam and Iris enter the kitchen.

BELINDA: (Belinda and Mrs. Emma stop what they are doing and greet Iris. Mr. Henry stands. Belinda and Iris run to each other as they giggle and hug.) "Mama and Daddy, this is my best friend…."

SAMUEL: "Hold it sis! It took me three months to get Miss Sarah to let Iris come to dinner. I want to be the one to introduce her. Mama and Daddy, this is my future wife, Iris Jackson."

MRS. EMMA: "Welcome to our home, Iris. Sam and Belinda have told us a lot of good things about you… you're as pretty as they said."

IRIS: "Thanks, Mrs. Emma. I've been looking forward to meeting y'all."

MR. HENRY: (Reaching to shake Iris' hand, but realizing he is holding a fried chicken leg) "This chicken leg is mine, but there's plenty more on the table. Now enough of this formality, let's sit down and enjoy all of this good food."

BELINDA: "Iris, sit next to me and Mama."

(Everyone except Sam sits at the table.)

MR. HENRY: "Sit down, son, and eat. Your Mama and sister have been cooking this food all morning." **(Sam finally sits.)**

MRS. EMMA: "Henry, will you say the grace?"

MR HENRY: (Mumbling some words) "Amen. Let's eat."

(They begin to pass the bowls and platters of food to each other. They fill their plates and begin to eat.)

MR. HENRY: "Iris, my wife is a great cook. She made the fried chicken, potato salad, sweet potato pie, and cornbread. You may want to pass on those collard greens; Belinda cooked them."

BELINDA: "Daddy!"

MRS. EMMA: (Laughing) "I cooked all the food; Belinda helped though."

IRIS: "The food is very good, Mrs. Emma."

MRS: EMMA: "Thank you. Do you want another piece of cornbread?"

IRIS: "Yes, ma'am."

MRS. EMMA: "Henry, will you pass Iris the cornbread?"

MR. HENRY: (Feeding the dog under the table) "You pass it. It's closer to you."

SAMUEL: "I'll get it for her, Mama." **(Sam holds the platter of cornbread for Iris to get another slice.)**

MR. HENRY: (Burping as he pushes away from the table, he reaches into his overalls pocket and pulls out a plug of chewing tobacco and takes a big bite. Everyone stops eating and looks at him.) "Dog and me is going to take a nap on the back porch." **(Mr. Henry and Dog leave the kitchen.)**

MRS. EMMA: "Sam, why don't you take Iris for a walk down to the creek?"

SAMUEL: "That's a good idea, Mama. **(Pause)** Iris, let's go. You'll love it down there."

BELINDA: "I'm going, too!"

MRS. EMMA: "No, Belinda. Let Sam and Iris have this time alone.

You can help me clean the kitchen."

(Sam and Iris exit the stage. Mrs. Emma and Belinda are left sitting at the table.)

MRS. EMMA: (Whispering to Belinda) "Sam wants to ask Iris to marry him. I gave him my grandmother's ring this morning."

BELINDA: "The ring with the name Rose engraved inside the band?"

MRS. EMMA: (Excited) "That's the ring!"

BELINDA: (Pouting) "I wanted you to give me that ring when I got married. I hope Iris says no."

MRS. EMMA: "You don't mean that. DO YOU?"

BELINDA: "NO…."

MRS. EMMA: "You can have my ring your daddy gave me."

BELINDA: "You promise?"

MRS. EMMA: "I promise."

(The stage lights dim to black)

SCENE 3

(It is later the same day. Mrs. Emma and Belinda are sitting in their small living room. Sam and Iris enter. Iris' clothes are a little disheveled.)

SAMUEL: "Mama, Iris accepted my proposal! She said she'd marry me when she finishes college. I know that sounds like a long ways off, but it's really not… because… I have another surprise for you and Belinda: I've enlisted in the army for two years."

MRS. EMMA: "Please don't go, Sam! You may get killed!"

SAMUEL: (Putting his arms around Mrs. Emma) "Oh, please don't look so sad, Mama. I'm going to be all right. I'll come home alive and well for you, Daddy, Belinda, and Iris—my future wife. By that time, Iris will be a teacher. While she teaches school, I'll build us a home near the creek and farm the land. I've always wanted to be a farmer. We already told Daddy our good news when we came up on the porch. He said Iris and I could have as much of his land as we need."

MRS. EMMA: "Have you told Miss Sarah?"

SAMUEL: (Going over to stand next to Iris. He puts his arm around her shoulders.) "We decided not to tell Miss Sarah right now. Iris wants to keep it a secret until she feels Miss Sarah can take the news."

BELINDA: "Iris, you and I are going to be sisters. How many children are you going to have?"

(Mrs. Emma and Sam laugh.)

SAMUEL: "It's too early to talk about children. I better get Iris home. I told Miss Sarah that I'd have her home by six o'clock. If I keep my word, Miss Sarah will let her come again."

IRIS: "Mrs. Emma, thank you for inviting me to dinner. I enjoyed meeting you and Mr. Henry. **(Showing off the ring on her finger)** Your grandma's ring is beautiful. I promise to wear it forever."

MRS. EMMA: (Holding Iris' hand so she and Belinda can get a closer look at the small gold ring.) "It fits like it was made for you. My grandmother would be honored for me to pass it on to you."

IRIS: "Thank you, Mrs. Emma. Just as soon as I get home, I'm going to hide it in my special keepsake box until I'm ready to tell Mama."

SAMUEL: "Iris, we better go."

IRIS: "Thank you again for supper. See you soon, Belinda."

(Sam and Iris exit the stage.)

(The stage lights dim to black)

SCENE 4

(It is later the same day. Iris and Samuel have arrived at Sarah's house. They enter through the kitchen.)

IRIS: Mama, I'm home. Where are you?

SARAH: I'm in the bedroom. Come on in.

IRIS: Sam is with me.

SARAH: It's okay. He can come in here, too. I'm decent.

(The lights dim on the kitchen as Iris and Samuel approach the bedroom. The lights then refocus on the bedroom.)

SAMUEL: "Miss Sarah, I told you I'd have Iris back by six and here she is."

SARAH: (Getting up from her rocking chair) "You did keep your promise, Sam. **(Pause)** It's getting late and we have a full day tomorrow. Iris, there's a dishpan of dirty dishes waiting for you in the kitchen."

SAMUEL: (Taking the hint) "Oh…I better be going then. **(Pause)** Miss Sarah, my parents said to tell you thanks for letting Iris come to dinner and they're looking forward to seeing her again."

SARAH: "They're welcome."

SAMUEL: "By the way, Miss Sarah, I've joined the army for two years. I'll be leaving for Korea in four weeks."

SARAH: "Well…good luck to you, Sam."

SAMUEL: "Thanks, Miss Sarah. **(Pause)** I'll see myself to the door. Iris, I'll see you next Sunday.

(Sam exits the stage.)

IRIS: "I better go and wash those dishes. **(Iris starts to exit, but pauses when Sarah speaks.)**

SARAH: "Wait, Iris! There's something I want to ask you. **(Iris pauses and returns to face Sarah, who now is sitting on the edge of her bed.)** Iris, what else did you and Sam do besides eat dinner?"

IRIS: "What do you mean?"

SARAH: "Iris, you know what I mean."

IRIS: "We didn't do ANYTHING, Mama!"

SARAH: "You're lying, Iris. You're not the same girl who left here this morning. I can tell just by looking at you. Sam has taken away your innocence and your dreams of being the first in the Jackson family to go to college and become somebody."

IRIS: "Mama… Sam loves me. He wouldn't do anything to hurt me or my family."

SARAH: "I hope you're right, but sometimes love is not enough. I feel a cold wind in your future." **(Sarah gets under her bed covers to take a nap.)**

IRIS: "Mama, before you go to sleep, there's something I've always wanted to ask you. I was just wondering, what is the name of your mama and daddy? In all of my life, I've never heard you talk about your parents. Were you the only child? Do you have brothers and sisters? **(Silence)** Mama, are you awake? **(Pause)** Mama, are you asleep?"

SARAH: (Sitting up and moving to the edge of her bed. Iris sits in the rocking chair.) "I don't know anything about my daddy except that he was a colored man. And I only remember a little about my mama and her family. I do know that they were white folks. My mama's first name was Rose. She was so pretty. I named your Aunt Rose after her. **(Pause)** I do remember early one morning when I was maybe four or five years old, Mama and two men—I believe they were my uncles—took me for a ride in a wagon pulled by two mules. I thought we were going to pick wild blackberries to can for pies and make jelly… but not this time. We eventually came upon a small shack where Mabel and Abraham Greene lived. They were a colored family. **(Pause)** My mama and uncles left me sitting in the wagon while they went inside to talk to Mabel and Abraham. When they returned, Mabel and Abraham were with them. **(Pause)** My mama was crying. One of my uncles lifted me off the wagon. Mama told me that she loved me, but she couldn't keep me any longer and I was to live with Mr. and Mrs. Green. **(Pause)** Mama tried to give me a wedding band inscribed with the name 'Rose', but one of my uncles stopped her. He said, 'No nigger's child is going to wear my grandmother's ring. That ring belongs in our white family.' **(Pause)** He then took the ring from my mama, put it in his pocket, and told Mama to stop crying."

IRIS: (Quickly glancing at the ring Samuel gave her before hiding it behind her back.) "Then, what did they do?"

SARAH: "They got back on the wagon and rode away. Mama didn't even kiss me goodbye or look back at me. I tried to run behind the wagon, but Mabel and Abraham stopped me and took me into their house."

IRIS: "What a sad story. Were Mabel and Abraham good to you?"

SARAH: "Mabel was the evilest woman I've ever known. She worked me like a slave from sunup to sundown. I cleaned their house, washed their clothes, and cooked all their meals. I was only allowed to eat the leftovers. I slept in a closet on top of old rags. I worked in the fields, planting and picking cotton, and fed the pigs. Sometimes I wished I would die. Mabel was a cold heartless woman, who never had a kind word to say to her husband, Abraham, or me. She never spoke to me unless she was telling me what she wanted me to do nor did she touch me unless she was giving me a whipping."

IRIS: "Was Abraham, just as evil as Mabel?"

SARAH: "Abraham was chicken shit when it came to Mabel. One day, I asked him why Mabel was so mean. He said she blamed him for their infant daughter's death. He thought taking me in would help, but it didn't. Sometimes, he would slip me extra morsels of food."

IRIS: "Sad! How long did you live with them?"

SARAH: "I lived with them for at least eight years, until one day a strange skinny white man came riding up to the house on his mule. Abraham was in the yard chopping firewood. I was in the garden cutting okra pods. The strange man got off his mule and talked to Abraham while his mule drank water from the trough. To this day, I can remember every word of their conversation.

(The stage lights dim on Sarah and Iris and refocus on the corner of the room where two men—an middle-aged white man, Mr. Parker James, and a middle-aged black man, Abraham Greene—will recreate the scene from Sarah's past. They begin to talk while Sarah and Iris

look on in silence.)

MR. PARKER JAMES: "Hey, Boy. What's your name?"

ABRAHAM GREEN: "Abraham Green, sir."

MR. PARKER JAMES: "Abraham, I'm Mr. Parker James. I'm letting my mule drink water from your trough. You don't mind, do you?"

ABRAHAM GREEN: "Not at all, sir. **(Pause)** Mister, if you don't mind me asking, where is you on your way to?"

MR. PARKER JAMES: "I'm on my way back to town. I rode out here in a wagon with a white family, who lives a mile or two down the road from your place. I came to buy this mule. I'm going to name her Sue. Don't you think that's a good name for a mule?"

ABRAHAM GREEN: "Yes, sir… Sue is a good name for a mule."

MR. PARKER JAMES: "Who's that white gal cutting okra over there?"

ABRAHAM GREEN: "She's not white. She just looks white. Her name is Sarah."

MR. PARKER JAMES: "Is she your daughter?"

ABRAHAM GREEN: "No, sir! My missus is as dark as I am."

MR. PARKER JAMES: "Where did she come from?"

ABRAHAM GREEN: "She's from a white family down the road from here. Her mama's family didn't want her because her daddy was colored. So they gave her to me and my missus."

MR. PARKER JAMES: "How old is she?"

ABRAHAM GREEN: "I'm not sure, sir. She was about five when we got her. She's been with us for about seven or eight years. You look like a kind man. Could you take her? **(Pause)** She's a good girl and a hard worker. She could clean your house, cook for you, and maybe you could teach her how to read and write."

MR. PARKER JAMES: "Will your missus let her go?"

ABRAHAM GREEN: "Yes, sir! She never cared for the girl, anyway." **(Abraham calls for Mabel.)** Mabel! Mabel! Come here! A man out here wants to ask you something." **(A middle-aged Mabel joins the two men.)**

ABRAHAM GREEN: "Mabel, this is Mr. Parker James. If it's alright with you, he said he'd take Sarah home with him."

MABEL GREEN: "I don't care. She's not my daughter. My daughter is dead." **(The stage lights dim on Mabel and the two men.**

They refocus on Sarah and Iris, who continue their conversation where it left off.)

SARAH: "Mr. James said, 'Girl you're coming home with me.' **(Pause)** He promised me that I would have a better life. **(Pause)** Right then, I left that knife and pan of okra sitting in the garden and without shoes on my feet and with just the clothes on my back, I mounted Mr. James' mule and we rode away. He took me to live in this same house we're sitting in now… to be his slave. Later, he moved into a small room in the back of his store. I stayed on in this house to raise y'all. Some of the things Parker James made me do… are not… even at your age… for your ears to hear. The only good thing Parker James gave me were my four children—John, Lilly, Cleo, and Rose. **(Sarah gets under her bed covers. With her back turned to Iris, she continues to speak.)** Sometimes I wonder which part of my life was worse. Was it with Mabel and Abraham or with Parker James?"

(The stage lights dim to black)

SCENE 5

SARAH: (Sitting in her rocking chair, reading a paperback mystery. Iris has just returned home from going with the Boggs to take Sam to the train station.) "You're back already? I guess the train station wasn't crowded."

IRIS: "It was very crowded. There was a long line of colored boys at the ticket window, but Mr. Henry and Sam were called to the front of the line. The white ticket taker just said, 'Move to the side boys and let this man buy his son a ticket.' **(Pause)** Mama, they just moved aside and didn't complain. They're going to fight for our country, too. Why were Sam and his daddy so special?"

SARAH: "Iris, do you really have to ask me that question? It was because the man thought Sam and Henry was white!"

IRIS: "Mama, will things ever change or will they always stay the same?"

SARAH: "I don't see a change in my lifetime, but mark my words… a change is going to come. There will be a time when you can be proud of the color of your skin and marry the person you love, whether they're white or colored. A white mother won't have to give her baby away just because the daddy was colored, like my mama had to give me away. One day a change will come. **(Pause)** Iris has it ever crossed your mind that your color is why Sam is attracted to you and why his parents accept you? **(Pause)** It's because you won't give them black grandbabies that won't be accepted by whites or coloreds."

IRIS: "Aunt Rose once told me that you wouldn't let her and Lilly date dark-skinned boys because you didn't want dark grandchildren. Mama, is Sam's color the reason you let him be my boyfriend?"

SARAH: "For the welfare of our children, we do what we have to do… not what we choose to do. Right now, that's the way it is. But like I say, a change is going to come."

IRIS: "When I write to Sam, I'm going to ask him if he would love me just as much if my skin was dark. For once, I'm going to prove you wrong."

SARAH: "Iris, it doesn't matter what Sam tells you. Sam won't be coming home anyway."

IRIS: "Please, Mama! Don't start with your bad luck predictions. Sam will come back home!"

SARAH: "I hope you're right! **(Pause)** I'm sorry, Iris. But, the chills I feel deep down in my bones are saying, 'No.' Iris, there are some hard days ahead for you… Only you can make the decision on how you'll handle them. **(Pause)** I just pray that one day in your far future… long after I'm dead… that you aren't still in Cross Town, Georgia—sitting in my rocking chair, crying about all the broken promises you made and those that were made to you."

(The stage lights dim to black)

SCENE 6

(Sarah anxiously waits for Iris to return home from school. She holds a letter that has arrived from the college to which Iris has applied. Before Sarah tells Iris about the letter, she needs to ask her if she is pregnant. Being a mother of four children, a grandmother, and a midwife—Sarah is an expert on the signs of pregnancy. She sees the signs in Iris. Sarah must know the truth from Iris. As Sarah waits, she paces, causing the loosened weatherworn floor to squeak under her large frame. Iris enters. From the look on Sarah's face, Iris knows Sarah has discovered her secret. It is time for her to confess that she is pregnant. It is going to devastate Sarah - and also Lilly - but she must tell them the truth before Mrs. Cora Mae does. Sarah stops pacing and sits in her rocking chair.)

SARAH: "Iris, you got a letter from that college you want to attend." **(Sarah gives the envelope to Iris, who anxiously opens the letter and reads it to herself.)**

IRIS: (Iris jumps up and down with joy.) "I've been accepted to college, Mama!"

SARAH: (Pointing to an extra chair for Iris to sit.) "Iris, sit with your grandma. I got something to ask you. **(Before sitting in the chair,**

facing Sarah, Iris sets her school books on her bed. She continues to grasp her acceptance letter. Sarah waits until Iris is seated before she begins to speak.) Iris, I'm going to come right out and ask you something and I want you to tell me the truth. **(Pause)** Iris, are you pregnant?"

IRIS: (Beginning to tear up) "Yes, Mama."

SARAH: (Jumping up from her seat with her hands clenched; She begins to pace the small bedroom. She is very angry and speaks loudly.) "I knew it! I knew it! You can't fool me! I said to myself that I better face the truth before it was too late to fix the problem. **(Sarah stops pacing and looks at Iris.)** About how far along are you?

IRIS: "I didn't have my period last month and I'm never late."

SARAH: (Raising her clenched fists high over her head and looking towards the ceiling.) "JESUS! JESUS! Help me JESUS! What are we going to do?"

IRIS: "Please, Mama. Let me explain Sam and my plans!"

SARAH: (Putting her clenched fists over her ears and loudly speaking.) "I don't want to hear it! I don't want to hear it! **(Sarah calms down for a moment and thinks.)** I got to find someone to go get Lilly. She needs to be here to hear this bad news!"

(Sarah runs off stage. She can be heard screaming for Mr. Jack Jones to stop his truck. She asks him to go and get Lilly. Iris remains sitting in her chair, looking helpless.)

SARAH: "Stop, Jack! **(Pause)** Jack, I need you to drive over to *Cleo's Place* and give Lilly a ride home. And hurry up!"

MR. JACK JONES: "Miss Jackson has someone died?"

SARAH: (Angrily) "Mind your own damn business! Just do what I say! Now go!" **(Sarah storms back into the bedroom. She stands with her arms folded as she talks to Iris.)**

SARAH: "I knew this would happen if you kept seeing that no good rascal, Sam Boggs. Now it's too late. **(Sarah goes over to where Iris sits. She cups Iris' chin into her large hand and holds her face close to hers. She speaks softly.)** Iris… baby… does anyone else know about this?"

IRIS: (Barely able to speak) "Sam, Belinda, Mr. and Mrs. Boggs, and… **(Hesitating)**

SARAH: "AND?"

IRIS: "Mrs. Cora Mae."

SARAH: (Releasing Iris's face) "Cora Mae! Cora Mae! That bitch knows? **(Sarah raises her hands to the heavens again.)** Lord JESUS, take me away! Pull me through one of these cracks… **(Looking down at the floor)** …and drag me straight to HELL! Now, it's all over Cross Town! That bitch, Cora Mae, got one up on me again! JESUS! JESUS! **(Pause)** Iris, you know how much I hate that bitch! Why did you tell her?"

IRIS: "I didn't. She just knew… like you did. She called me up to her desk and asked me and…."

SARAH: "And you just HAD to tell her the truth!"

(Lilly hurries inside. She is wearing her waitress uniform, an apron, and a shabby purse with its strap across her shoulder. She has a worried look on her face. She looks at Sarah, who is standing nearby, and then over at Iris, who is sitting in the chair. She then speaks.)

LILLY: "Mama, what's wrong? **(Silence)** Will one of you tell me something? I couldn't get anything out of Mr. Jack. He just kept shaking his head and saying, **(Mocking Mr. Jones)** 'I don't know. I don't know! Your mama just says for me to get you home right away!' **(Silence)** Is somebody dead? Who died?"

"SARAH: "No one is dead! **(Exhausted, Sarah sits in her rocking chair.)** Iris has something to tell you."

LILLY: (Looking at Iris) "Iris, what is it?"

(Silence)

SARAH: (Loudly) "Tell her Iris or I will!"

LILLY: "Iris, will you please tell me before I drop dead!'"

SARAH: (Interrupting) "I'll tell you! Iris is going to have Sam Boggs' baby!"

LILLY: "Iris, is this true?"

IRIS: "It's true."

(Lilly sits on the edge of the bed, looking stunned. She puts her hand on her chest as if she were having a heart attack.)

LILLY: "Iris, how could you? How could you do this to us? **(Turning to Sarah)** What are we going to do?"

SARAH: (Shaking her head) "I don't know! I don't know!"

IRIS: (Begging) "Please listen to me. I'm going to graduate from Mrs. Cora Mae's School in less than two months. The baby will be born before I leave for college. Sam has already written to his mama and daddy and told them about our situation. Mrs. Emma wrote back and told him that the day I finish school, I can come and live with them. When the baby is born—Mrs. Emma, Mr. Henry, and Belinda will raise the baby while I finish college. By that time, Sam will be out of the Army and I'll be a teacher. We'll get married and raise our child. By then, who will care about what happened two or three years ago?"

LILLY: (Agreeing) "Well, Mama… that's the best we can do."

SARAH: "I know someone who can fix this problem!"

LILLY: (Adamantly) "Mama, if you're thinking what I think you're thinking, the answer is NO! **(Pause)** NO! This baby will be your great, great, grandchild and my grandchild. Who knows what a great person this baby will become? Besides… we're not the only ones who know about this baby. Sam knows and his family knows. What lie would we tell them if this baby just disappeared? **(Pause)** Iris... besides us and the Boggs, have you told anyone else?"

IRIS: "Mrs. Cora Mae knows."

SARAH: "Now the whole town knows."

LILLY: (Hugging Iris) "Don't worry, Iris. We'll get through this somehow."

SARAH: "Iris, your dreams of going to college, becoming a teacher, and marrying Sam won't come to pass. I feel a cold chill deep down in my bones."

LILLY: "Iris, don't listen to Mama's predictions. They won't come true. Not this time… Not this time. I promise!”

(The stage lights dim to black)

ACT IV

SCENE 1

(Iris and Belinda have graduated from Mrs. Cora Mae's School. Sarah, Lilly, and Cleo have driven Iris to the Boggs' house where Iris will live until the baby is born. The Jacksons were invited to stay for dinner so the two families can get to know each other better. The Jacksons and Boggs have finished eating dinner and are sitting on the back porch. Dog, the old hound, lies nearby. Iris and Belinda are in Belinda's bedroom. They are sitting on her bed that has a pink chenille bedspread. A baby crib sits in the corner of the room. There is a tattered teddy bear inside of it. Iris and Belinda are talking while looking at baby clothes that she and Mrs. Emma made as well as the crib that Mr. Henry built for the baby.)

BELINDA: "Mama and I sewed these things for the baby."

IRIS: "They are so cute! Thank you, Belinda."

BELINDA: "I'm glad you like them. **(Looking over at the crib)** Daddy made the crib."

(Iris goes over to admire the crib. She takes the tattered teddy bear out of it and holds it tightly against her chest just like she use to hold Miss Ann.)

BELINDA: "The teddy bear is mine. I'll let the baby play with it. Daddy wants a grandson. Mama and I hope it's a girl."

IRIS: "I hope it's a girl, too."

BELINDA: (Looking at Iris) "If you get any fatter, I'll have to let you have my whole bed while I sleep on the floor."

IRIS: (Laying the teddy bear back into the crib and putting her hands on her hips) "I'm not getting fat! It's the baby inside of my stomach. When the baby comes, I'm going to be my skinny self again. **(They laugh as Iris again sits on the bed next to Belinda.)** Thanks, Belinda… for all you, Mr. Henry, and Mrs. Emma are doing for me and the baby."

BELINDA: "You're welcome. After all, it's going to be my niece or nephew. Lord, please, let it be a girl! **(Pause)** Iris, did you know you could get pregnant when you and Sam were doing it?"

IRIS: "I guess so."

BELINDA: "Why did you do it then?"

IRIS: (Looking perplexed) "I don't know."

BELINDA: "Didn't Lilly tell you about the birds and the bees?"

IRIS: "Yes, but I guess she didn't tell me enough because the bee that stung me gave me a ba-bee."

BELINDA: "Now, that's funny."

IRIS: "Have you?"

BELINDA: (Curious) "Have I what?"

IRIS: "You know, been stung by a bee?"

BELINDA: "No… No! But, I want to be stung someday. Did it feel good?"

IRIS: "Not at first, but after I kept doing it, I got to liking it."

BELINDA: "I guess it depends on the bee."

IRIS: "Let's go out on the porch and see if our folks are getting along. We'll have plenty of time to talk later."

(The stage lights dim to black)

SCENE 2

(Mr. Henry, Mrs. Emma, Sarah, and Lilly are sitting in old woven-cane chairs at the Boggs' house. Cleo is sitting on the edge of the porch, chewing tobacco, and spitting it in an empty vegetable can. Mr. and Mrs. Boggs are making ice cream in a hand-cranked churn. Mr. Henry turns the crank while Mrs. Emma adds chunks of ice.)

MR. HENRY: "My old lady and me are glad you could come to dinner. It's good to meet our future grandbaby's other side of the family."

MRS. EMMA: "Thank you Sarah for bringing the extra food."

SARAH: "Glad to help since y'all will have an extra mouth to feed."

LILLY: "If we can help out more just let us know."

MRS. EMMA: "Thanks Lilly, but we have plenty of food. We have jars and jars of canned vegetables, meats, and fish. With all this land we own, you can say that we are very rich poor folks."

CLEO: "On our way down here, I was telling Mama and Lilly that these woods look very familiar. I believe I've trapped in these woods."

MR. HENRY: "My family owned acres and acres of land down here. My older brother, Jim, and I inherited all this land that our great, great, grandparents and parents owned. A lot of colored farmhands lived in those houses, but only chimneys are left standing now."

SARAH: "I told Cleo that I believe I once lived on this land. One of the old places we passed, driving down here, looked just like the house where I lived as a child. My mama was white and my daddy was colored. When I was a small child, my white side of the family gave me away to a colored family."

MR: HENRY: "Sarah, who did they give you to?"

SARAH: "They gave me to a colored family by the name of Mabel and Abraham Green.

MR. HENRY: "Emma and I can relate to your story. Emma's mama and daddy lived on our land and worked for my grandparents until my grandparents died. Then they came to work for my mama and daddy. That's when I first saw my beautiful Emma. Before then, I didn't know they had a child. Emma grew up in our house. When her parents died, Emma stayed on and worked for us. By then, we were adults and Emma and I had fallen in love. After my racist daddy died, we decided to stop hiding our feelings for each other and tell my mama that we were in love and wanted to go somewhere—where no one would know Emma was colored so we could get married. We were hoping Mama wasn't a bigot, like my daddy, and would give us her blessings, but we were very wrong."

MRS. EMMA: "His mama laid her hand on my stomach and said, 'If my son marries you nigger, may every son you birth die.' **(Pause)** It has come true once. **(Pause)** I don't know if I could go on living if something ever happened to my Sam."

(There is a loud knock at the front door, just as Iris and Belinda join the family on the back porch.)

MR. HENRY: "Who could that be knocking on the front door?"

BELINDA: "I'll get it, Daddy."

(Belinda exits the stage while the others wait in suspense. Belinda returns with two male soldiers in uniform; one is White and the other one is Black. The soldiers follow Belinda to the back porch. The Black soldier has an envelope in his hand.)

BELINDA: "Daddy, these soldiers are here to see you and Mama."

MR. HENRY: (Stuttering) "I'm Henry Boggs. **(He points towards Mrs. Emma)** This is my wife, Emma. Are you here about my son, Sam?"

MRS. EMMA: (Interrupting) "Is Sam badly hurt? When will he be well enough to come home?"

BLACK SOLDIER: "Mrs. Boggs… **(Pause)** I wish the news was that good… but your son is dead."

(Sarah and Lilly begin to cry. Belinda jumps up and runs, screaming off stage. Dog follows behind her. Iris stands in shock.)

MR. HENRY: "My son is dead?"

WHITE SOLDIER: "Yes, sir. He was killed on the battlefield. He served our country well. Your family has our deepest sympathy."

MRS. EMMA: (Screaming) "No! No! Not my Sam!"

(Cleo jumps up from where he is sitting and catches Mrs. Emma as she faints. Cleo carries her off stage. Sarah and Lilly follow them. Only Mr. Henry and Iris remain on the porch with the soldiers. The Black soldier hands Mr. Henry the envelope.)

BLACK SOLDIER: "Again, you have our deepest sympathy."

(The soldiers exit the back porch. Mr. Henry and Iris are alone on the porch.)

MR. HENRY: (Squeezing the envelope in his hand as he walks over to Iris.) "Iris, don't you worry. You're a part of this family. We'll get through this. You can rely on us to keep the promise we made to you and Sam."

(Iris begins to sob. Mr. Henry takes a rag, which he uses for a handkerchief, from his back pocket and hands it to her. She wipes her

tears with it. He puts his arm around her shoulders.)

MR HENRY: "Take care of that baby you're carrying. **(Pause)** That's all we got left of my son."

(The stage lights dim to black)

SCENE 3

(It has been several weeks since Sam's funeral. Iris and Belinda are lying in bed at the Boggs' house. Iris is rereading the last letter she received from Sam.)

BELINDA: "Iris, please read Sam's letter out loud so I can hear it."

IRIS: "NO! It's personal!"

BELINDA: (looking pitiful) "PLEASE."

IRIS: "Well, just this time."

(Iris and Belinda hold their positions. Iris continues to hold the letter as if she is reading it aloud. Belinda looks on attentively. However, the actor that has played Sam thus far will read the letter aloud from off stage. As they remain motionless, the audience will hear his voice.)

"My Dearest Iris,

It's so lonely over here in this God-forsaken place. I dream of the day when I'm home with you and my baby. Daddy hopes the baby will be a boy, so he can continue the Boggs' family name. Mama, Belinda, and I want the baby to be a girl. Whether the baby is a boy or girl, I'm happy that you... the woman I love... will be the mother of my child."

(The male voice stops reading the letter as Iris and Belinda hear noises

coming from Mr. and Mrs. Boggs' bedroom. They slightly move to signify the change in the scene. They each put one hand to one of their ears and listen.)

BELINDA: "Mama is crying herself to sleep again. **(Pause)** Go ahead and finish Sam's letter." **(Before Iris could continue to read Sam's letter, Mr. Henry enters the room. Iris and Belinda sit up in bed.)**

MR. HENRY: (Looking tired and already dressed) "Emma finally went to sleep."

BELINDA: "Daddy… is Mama going to be alright?"

MR. HENRY: (Shaking his head) "She's getting worse. She eats just enough to have the strength to walk down to the family cemetery everyday. She just sits by Sam's grave and cries. She's become very frail. She's going to mourn herself to death… like Dog did. That faithful hound would go to sniff Sam's grave everyday until we found him dead on top of Sam's grave. **(Pause)** I can't let that happen to Emma, too. **(Pause)** I got to get Emma some help before it's too late. **(Pause)** Her sisters want me to bring her to Detroit. They want her to see a doctor that specializes in her condition. But, I can't leave you girls down here alone. **(Pause)** Iris, do you think Sarah would come and stay with y'all?"

IRIS: "She might…."

BELINDA: "Don't you worry, Daddy. If Miss Sarah can't stay, Iris and I can take care of ourselves until you and Mama get back."

MR. HENRY: "I can't leave two teenage girls, one pregnant, down here alone in these woods for days and nights with only a kerosene lamp. Dog isn't here to protect y'all either. GOD only knows what kind of wild animals or escaped convicts are living in these woods. How would you get food or firewood for the stove? What if you or Iris gets sick… or worse… what if the baby comes early?"

BELINDA: "I didn't think about that."

MR. HENRY: "Well, I did. That's why I'm going to Sarah's house to ask her if she'll stay with y'all. If you girls be very quiet, Emma may sleep until I return."

IRIS: (Pleading) "Mr. Henry, please convince Mama to come and stay with us."

MR. HENRY: "I'm going to do my best."

(The stage lights dim to black)

SCENE 4

(Mr. Henry knocks at Sarah's door. She comes to the door and looks surprised to see him.)

SARAH: "Has the baby come?"

MR. HENRY: "No, ma'am. Iris and Belinda are fine, but Emma is doing poorly. She's about to lose her mind since Sam died. I got to get her some help before it's too late."

SARAH: "Come on in, Henry. **(Mr. Henry goes inside.)** Have a seat. **(Mr. Henry and Sarah sit.)** I know what Emma is going through. I lost my son, John, to World War II. It seems just like yesterday when I received the bad news. **(Pause)** I was at work, at Mr. James' store, when two soldiers—one white and one colored—just like the two who came to your house, walked in. It was the first time a colored person, except for me, used the front door. Everyone in the store knew they had to be looking for me. Only two families in Cross Town had sons fighting in the war… the Rutledge family, who are white… and mine. They had already gotten word that their son was killed so the soldiers had to be there for me. **(Pause)** I know what Emma is feeling. I don't know what I would do if I lost my Cleo, too."

MR. HENRY: "Thanks, Sarah, for understanding what I'm going through. I'm planning on taking Emma to Detroit tomorrow to see a special doctor…."

SARAH: (Interrupting) "What about Iris and Belinda? Who'll be there to care for them? What if the baby comes before you and Emma get back?"

MR. HENRY: "That's the reason I'm here. I want to ask you for your help."

SARAH: "How can I help?"

MR. HENRY: "Will you please come down to the house and stay with Belinda and Iris until Emma and me come back home. If the baby comes, will you know what to do?"

SARAH: (Boastfully) "I sure will. I basically brought my children and Iris into this world all by myself."

MR. HENRY: "Sarah, can I count on you? **(Pause)** I'll use your address to send letters to Belinda, so y'all know how we're doing and when we're returning."

SARAH: "Henry, it's a bad time for me to leave my house. My son, Cleo—you met him when we were at your house—is in a bad situation. He may end up in a lot of trouble and need me to rescue him. **(Pause)**

Henry… being the grandfather of my future great grandchild… I consider you family, so I can be frank and confide in you. I need to talk to someone. **(Pause)** Cleo has started to hang around Colored Alley with those street-smart people and city slickers. **(Pause)** Cleo has lived most of his life in the woods… hunting and fishing. Even though he's used the money from selling animal skins to buy him a café… he's still a mama's boy at heart. **(Pause)** Cleo's not used to the fast life in Cross Town. He has become smitten with the town's whore, Miss Wilma Lee. She makes her living having sex with any man who has a dollar in his pocket and Cleo foolishly thinks she loves him. Henry, if my dumb, backwoods, high-tempered, thirty-year old son… who has never had a girlfriend, keeps messing with that woman… he's going to end up in prison for killing her or with a disease! So you see my situation."

MR. HENRY: (Standing to leave) "I understand your dilemma… I'll try to think of something else."

SARAH: (Standing) "Wait, Henry! I can't let those two girls stay alone in those woods to be eaten by wolves and mountain lions or taken advantage of by hunters and escaped convicts. I can't let my great grandbaby be born without an adult around who knows what to do. I'll stay with them and pray that you and Emma will return soon."

MR. HENRY: Thank you Miss Sarah. I promise Emma and I will return soon.

(The stage lights dim to black)

SCENE 5

(Iris is sitting at the kitchen table in the Boggs' house. Belinda is washing dishes. Sarah is fishing at the creek.)

IRIS: "How long have Mr. Henry and Mrs. Emma been gone?"

BELINDA: "Just five weeks."

IRIS: "Mama is getting restless. She's ready to go home. The only thing keeping her here is being able to fish at the creek everyday… or talking with Lilly when she brings the mail and groceries… and because Uncle Cleo has stayed out of trouble."

BELINDA: "Daddy keeps saying, 'Soon, soon, soon.'"

IRIS: (Grabbing her stomach and screaming in pain) "Oh! My stomach hurts! **(Breaking into laughter)** It's those collards you cooked. I told Mama not to let you cook supper!"

BELINDA: (Defiantly) "There was nothing wrong with those greens! They didn't make Miss Sarah and me sick. You just ate too many."

IRIS: "How do you know? Mama could be down at the creek dying, right now."

(Iris and Belinda begin to laugh loudly until they see water coming from under Iris' dress, making a puddle on the floor.)

BELINDA: “Girl, what’s wrong with you?”

IRIS: (Crying out) “I don’t know!”

BELINDA: “Are you having the baby?”

IRIS: “I must be! Go get Mama! Tell her the baby is coming! Hurry, Belinda!”

(Belinda drops the plate that she is holding and dashes out the door.)

SCENE 6

(It is later the same day. Sarah and Belinda rush into the kitchen. They find Iris and her baby lying on the kitchen floor. She has given birth to a baby girl.)

BELINDA: (Stunned) "Oh My God! Iris… you've had the baby. Miss Sarah…."

SARAH: "Belinda, get me some towels while I tend to Iris and the baby!" **(Belinda quickly exits the stage and immediately returns with some towels. Sarah takes the baby from Iris' arms and wraps her in a towel.)**

SARAH: "Belinda, while I hold the baby… you help Iris to the bedroom."

(Belinda helps Iris off the floor. As they exit, Belinda looks back at Sarah, who is holding the small bundle in her arms.)

BELINDA: "Is it a boy or girl?"

SARAH: "It's a girl."

IRIS: "I'm going to name her Samantha."

(The stage lights go dark for forty-five seconds or less. When the lights come back on, the same scene continues from the bedroom. Iris

lies in bed, exhausted. Sarah carries the baby, wrapped in a towel, and places her in Iris' arms. Iris, who is noticeably weak, holds the baby to her chest. Belinda sits in a chair by the bed. Lilly enters the bedroom, carrying a letter that Mr. Henry mailed to Belinda. Lilly is shocked to see that the baby has arrived.)

SARAH: "Lilly, you're just in time to meet your new granddaughter."

BELINDA: (Excitedly) "Iris named her Samantha after Sam!"

LILLY: (Walking over to the bed to check on Iris and the new baby.) "Iris, how do you feel?"

IRIS: "I feel alright."

(Lilly takes a closer look at the baby. She carefully removes the towel from around the baby's face.)

LILLY: "Mama, she's so pretty! She looks white! Do you think she's going to stay this color?"

SARAH: "I hope so."

(Lilly finally hands Belinda the letter from Mr. Henry. Belinda opens the envelope, removes the letter, and silently reads the contents. Sarah, Lilly, and Iris wait for her to share the news.)

BELINDA: (Sadly) "Daddy said the doctors told him that Mama will never recover from her mental illness. He wants me to close the house, pack everything I can bring with me, and come to Detroit. He needs me to help Aunt Bea and Aunt Helen care for Mama. Daddy says to tell you that he's sorry how things turned out… but he promises that he will see his grandchild, one day. **(Pause)** I'm sorry, Iris, but what can I do?"

IRIS: "There's nothing you can do, but go to Detroit and help take care of Mrs. Emma. Samantha and I will have to go home with Mama and Lilly. I'll work at Uncle Cleo's cafe and raise my child."

SARAH: "Belinda, when do you think you'll be ready to leave?"

BELINDA: "In a week or two."

LILLY: "Good! That will give Iris more time down here to heal."

BELINDA: "Miss Lilly, will you drive me to the train station when it's time for me to go?"

LILLY: "I'll be glad to, Belinda. We'll all leave this house together."

(The stage lights dim to black)

SCENE 7

(Iris is back home in Sarah's bedroom. She is sitting in Sarah's rocking chair and holding her new baby girl, Samantha. Samantha has colic and her crying has kept Iris up all night. Iris begins to doze just as Cleo walks in the door.)

CLEO: "Good morning, Iris. You look like you had a bad night."

IRIS: "I did, Uncle Cleo. Samantha has the colic."

CLEO: Hope she feels better by tonight so you can get some sleep."

IRIS: "I hope so, too."

CLEO: "Is Mama and Lilly in the kitchen?"

IRIS: "Yes, sir."

(Cleo goes into the kitchen. From where Iris sits, she hears every word of Cleo, Sarah, and Lilly's conversation.)

SARAH: "Good morning, Cleo."

CLEO: "Good morning, Mama."

LILLY: "Cleo, you're too early. I'm not ready, yet!"

SARAH: "Son, sit down and have a cup of coffee. I'll cook you some grits and scrambled eggs."

CLEO: (Sits down at the table) "Thanks, Mama. I could use a cup of coffee."

SARAH: "Son, you look jittery. Is there something on your mind?"

CLEO: "Yes, Mama."

SARAH: "Son, what is it? You can tell, Mama."

CLEO: "Mama… Lilly… I've decided to ask Wilma Lee to marry me."

SARAH: (Loudly) "Cleo, have you lost your mind? Don't you know that slut has slept with just about every colored and white man in Cross Town, Georgia?"

CLEO: (Loudly) "That was in her past! She has changed!"

SARAH: "Fool, don't you see what Wilma Lee is doing? If Wilma Lee—that skinny, yellowtail harlot, and gold-digging bitch—marries you, it's because she wants *Cleo's Place* for herself! The place that I helped you buy so you could have something when I die!"

CLEO: (Angrily) "Mama, I bought *Cleo's Place* with the money I earned from selling animal pelts! *Cleo's Place* is mine!"

SARAH: "Lilly, see if you can talk some sense into your brother's head."

LILLY: (Calmly) "Cleo, the only reason Wilma Lee gives you the time of day is because you own that café. It's the talk of the town. Everyone knows… but you."

CLEO: "You're lying!"

LILLY: (Calmly) "It's true, Cleo. **(Pause)** We just didn't want to hurt you. **(Pause)** We had hoped the feelings you have for Wilma Lee would've blow over by now."

SARAH: (Placing a cup of coffee in front of Cleo. He begins to take sips.) "I don't want that whore to be a part of this family! So stop being a fool… FOOL!"

CLEO: (He begins to shout.) "Mama, don't keep calling me a fool! I'm tired of you calling me a fool! I'm thirty years old, and I'm not a child or a fool! **(He throws the coffee cup onto the floor.)** When I leave from here, I'm going over to Wilma's house and ask her to marry me! **(Pause)** There's nothing you or Lilly can do to stop me!"

LILLY: (Shouting) "Cleo, I can guarantee you this… if you marry that whore, I won't continue to work for you at *Cleo's Place*. Wilma Lee will NOT be my boss!"

CLEO: "You don't have to work for me! I don't need you! My wife, Wilma Lee, can run *Cleo's Place*!"

LILLY: (Shouting) "I'm not coming to work today, either!"

CLEO: "I don't give a damn! You and Mama can go to Hell!"

SARAH: (Shouting) "Cleo, leave my house now! **(Pause)** If you don't get that foolish idea out of your mind about marrying that slut, don't come back!"

CLEO: "I won't!"

SARAH: "You'll be back. I feel a cold, cold chill deep in my bones."

CLEO: "To hell with your fortune-telling bones!" **(Cleo storms out of the kitchen. He quickly exits the stage.)**

(The stage lights dim to black)

SCENE 8

(It is later the same day. Sarah, Lilly, and Iris are in the kitchen. They are sitting at the table. Iris is breast-feeding Samantha. Sarah and Lilly are snapping a pan of green beans for dinner. Cleo storms into the kitchen. He is crying and has a terrified look on his face. He has a shotgun in his hand and blood splatted on his overalls. As soon as Iris sees him, she takes Samantha and runs out of the kitchen. Sarah rises slowly from her chair to confront Cleo. Lilly is too afraid to move.)

LILLY: (Screaming) Mama! He's got a gun!

SARAH: "Son, don't do something you'll regret! **(She calmly reaches for the shotgun.)** Give me the gun."

(Cleo hands the shotgun to Sarah. She takes it and carefully puts it in a corner of the kitchen. Cleo continues to cry and fidget.)

SARAH: "Cleo, what have you done? Please stop crying and tell Mama so I can help you!"

CLEO: "You and Lilly was right!"

SARAH: "We were right about what?"

CLEO: "You were right about Wilma Lee!"

SARAH: "Cleo, did you do something bad to Wilma?"

CLEO: (Crying out loud) "Mama, I killed her! **(Pause)** I killed her!"

SARAH: (Shocked by the news, she sits down hard in her chair) "Cleo, please tell me it's not true!"

CLEO: "Mama, it's true! I killed Wilma Lee. **(Pause)** She's dead!"

LILLY: "Why, Cleo?"

CLEO: "Because I went over to her house, opened her door, and went to her bedroom. There she was! **(Pause)** Mama, I found Wilma in bed with that old white man, David Poole! They were naked and doing it!"

LILLY: "David Poole? That hick you sell catfish to?"

CLEO: "That's him!"

LILLY: "Why didn't you just leave?"

CLEO: "I was about to until Wilma Lee called me a fool and told me to get the hell out of her house. **(Pause)** Something just snapped inside of me. **(Pause)** I went out to my truck, got my shotgun, and went back into her bedroom. **(Pause)** I was going to kill them both, but Mr. Poole jumped out the window and ran. **(Pause)** Wilma started to scream, **(Mimicking Wilma Lee)** 'Please don't shoot me! Please don't shoot me!' So I beat her with the butt of my shotgun until her head was a bloody mess."

LILLY: (Hopeful) "She may still be alive!"

SARAH: (Breathless) "Whether she is or not, we got to get Cleo out of town before Wilma Lee's body is found! Parker James isn't alive to help get us out of trouble anymore… so Lilly you'll have to. **(Pause)** I'll be damned if I'm going to let my son go to prison. **(Pause)** Your brother will never survive living in a small prison cell, twiddling his thumbs until he goes mad… **(Pause)** just because he killed a WHORE! **(Pause)** My Cleo was born to be a free man!"

LILLY: "What if Mr. Poole went to Sheriff Goodson and reported Cleo? He and his deputies might've already been to Wilma Lee's house and be on their way here."

SARAH: "If Poole told Sheriff Goodson, he and his vigilantes would've already been here dragging Cleo away. That married white man won't tell anybody that he was with a colored whore or name Cleo as her killer. **(Looking at Cleo, who can't stop moving.)** Cleo! Stop fidgeting! Go out to the truck, lie down in the back, and wait for me and Lilly!"

CLEO: "Mama, what are you going to do?"

SARAH: (Standing and putting her hand on Cleo's shoulder) "I'm not going to let anybody hurt you, Son. **(Pause)** So trust Mama. **(Pause)** Lilly and I are going to drive you to *Cleo's Place* and help you pack some of your things to take with you. **(Pause)** Then we're going to drive you as far as we can into the back woods so you can lose yourself in the wilderness. **(Pause)** Don't try to contact us because they may spy on us. **(Pause)** People know that you knew Wilma… so don't come back to Cross Town. **(Pause)** You know I love you, Son… so take care of yourself!"

CLEO: "I love you, too, Mama. I love all of you. I'm sorry for causing you all this trouble. To make up for it, **(Pause)** Lilly, I want you to have *Cleo's Place* and my truck. **(Pause)** Mama, the rest of my money's hidden in the bottom of my old tool chest—it's yours. **(Pause)** Tell Iris goodbye and I'm sorry I scared her and Samantha. **(Pause)** Mama, someway… somehow… I promise to let you know that I'm alive."

LILLY: (Crying) "Thank you, Cleo. I love you and I will take care of *Cleo's Place*."

SARAH: "We all love you! **(Getting back in control of the situation)** Now do what I told you! Go and hide in the back of the truck."

(Cleo quickly exits the stage.)

SARAH: "Lilly, go and get Iris. Tell her that it's safe to bring Samantha back in the house. **(Pause)** Tell Iris I want her to stay in the house… and if anyone comes by asking for Cleo or asking where he is… to say that she doesn't know! **(Pause)** I'll be waiting for you in the truck."

(Lilly and Sarah leave the stage at the same time, exiting from two different directions.)

(The stage lights dim to black)

ACT V

SCENE 1

(It is fifteen years later. Samantha is enjoying her high-school graduation dinner with her family. Sarah, Lilly, and Iris have noticeably aged.)

SARAH: "Samantha, we're so proud of you being the first colored valedictorian of an integrated school."

IRIS: "And the youngest person to graduate."

SARAH: "And you will be our first college graduate in the family!"

LILLY: "I knew she was going to be the one to make the Jackson family proud."

SAMANTHA: "Thanks everyone. **(Pause)** Finally… I can get away from this backwards town and its 'yes, sir' and 'yes, ma'am' colored people."

(There is knock at the door.)

SARAH: (Loudly) "Come in."

(Mr. Jack Jones enters. He has a small package in his hand. He keeps his eyes on Sarah as he slowly walks over to where Iris sits.)

MR. JACK JONES: "Good afternoon ladies. I hope I'm not disturbing your dinner."

LILLY: "No, sir… **(Pause)** Mr. Jones, Samantha graduated from high school today at the top of her class and we're having a celebration dinner. There's plenty of food. Would you like to join us?"

MR. JACK JONES: "No thank you, Miss Lilly. **(Pause)** Congratulations, Samantha. What a coincidence! When I was in Detroit a few days ago to visit my daughter, Evelyn… I saw and talked to your Aunt Belinda. **(Pause)** As a matter of fact, Belinda is the reason I'm at your house today. She wanted me to deliver this package to you and Samantha." **(Mr. Jack Jones hands the package to Iris.)**

IRIS: (Excited to receive news from an old friend; she quickly accepts the package.) "You talked to Belinda Boggs?"

MR. JACK JONES: "I sure did! She told me to make sure you get this package."

IRIS: "Thank you, Mr. Jones."

SARAH: "Jack, are you sure you don't want something to eat? **(Jokingly)** I won't bite you."

MR. JONES: "No thank you, Miss Sarah. Ladies, y'all have a good day."

SARAH: "You, too."

(Mr. Jones exits the stage. Iris opens the package. Inside, she finds a land deed and a letter from Belinda. It is addressed to Iris and Samantha.)

IRIS: "Samantha… your Aunt Belinda wrote me and you a letter. Do you want to read it first?"

SAMANTHA: "You can read it for both of us."

SARAH: "For goodness sake… will one of you just read the letter?"

IRIS: "Okay… I'll read it out loud so we all can hear."

(Sarah, Lilly, and Samantha hold their positions. They are all looking at Iris as she glances down at the letter and scans it as though she is reading it. However, the person who has played Belinda thus far will read the letter from off stage. The audience will only hear her voice. The only person that will move is Iris, who will occasionally turn the pages to coincide with the person who is doing the reading from off stage.)

"Dearest Iris,

I can't believe it's been fifteen years since you, baby Samantha, and I went our separate ways. Yesterday on my way to work, I ran into Mr. Jack Jones. He was up here visiting his relatives—Mrs. Cora Mae, Evelyn, and

Annie. Mrs. Cora Mae lives with Evelyn in the tenement across the street from where Annie and I live. I'm giving this important package to Mr. Jack to give to you. He said he would and I trust him.

Mrs. Cora Mae is very sick and has mellowed since she was our teacher. She said to tell you hello. Annie is suffering with cancer. She said to tell you hello and to make sure I told you that she was wrong and sorry for what she did to you years ago. She said you'd know what she was talking about.

I'm sorry I dropped out of your life when you were having such a difficult time, but life hasn't been too kind to me either. Mama is still alive and lives in an institution for the insane. Even though she does not recognize me anymore, I go and visit her every Sunday. Her doctor said that she would never return to a normal life.

Five years after we moved to Detroit, Daddy died of a broken heart. He never got over Sam's death and learning that Mama would never be her old self again. Daddy was so proud that you named Samantha after Sam. He always planned to come home and visit his granddaughter, but with Mama's neediness—he never found the time. Daddy's brother, Mr. Jim, begged me to let him pay for Daddy's body to be returned to Cross Town so he could be buried next to Sam. So, I did.

Mr. Jim wants me to call him Uncle Jim. He said he has one foot in the grave and wants me to forgive him for the way he treated Daddy and us so he can go to Heaven and be with Daddy and Sam... and I did. It's amazing how getting old, and being about to die, can change a person.

I should have come to see you and Samantha when I brought Daddy's body home, but I had become bitter. For a long time, I blamed you for my family's bad luck. I'm much older now and know better than that.

After saying all of this, my most important reason for writing this letter is to let you know what I did for you and Samantha. With Daddy being dead and Mama spending the rest of her life in an asylum... and since I don't plan to return to Cross Town to live, I have made you and Samantha the new owners of our old homestead and all of the land that we own. **(Iris shows the deeds to Lilly and Sarah, who are wiping their teary eyes with their dinner napkins. They hold this position as the voice from off stage continues to read the letter.)**

Take this gift from my family and build you, Samantha, Miss Lilly, and Miss Sarah a home. My only wish is that you care for Sam and Daddy's graves... and just in case... upon our deaths, save two plots for Mama and me.

Love,

Belinda"

SARAH: (About to cry) "That was very kind of Belinda."

LILLY: (Still wiping her eyes) "It sure was."

IRIS: (Elated at first, but quickly saddened.) "I thought Belinda had forgotten about us, but I was wrong. What a great graduation gift from your Aunt Belinda. **(Pause)** Now, you can return to Cross Town after you graduate from college, teach school, and build you a home on the land of your ancestors."

SAMANTHA: (Defiantly) "I told you! I don't ever want to make my home in Cross Town, Georgia. As soon as I get my teacher's degree, I am going to move to a big city like New York and teach school. I will marry me a rich man and if I don't want to work, my husband can take care of our children and ME! I don't want to be poor all of my life and grow old, tired, ugly, and gray like you, Lilly, and Mama!"

LILLY: (Disappointed) "Samantha, you're very young. As you get older, you'll see things differently."

SAMANTHA: "I don't think so!" **(She gets up from the table and exits the stage.)**

IRIS: "Samantha is right. **(She looks over at Sarah and then at Lilly.)** We have just let ourselves go and are becoming fat, unattractive, tired, old, graying women. There's nothing exciting in our lives, anymore.

All we do is work. We're not that old, but I can't remember the last time a man gave me a second look or asked me out on a date. For the last fifteen years, I've done nothing but devote all my time to raising Samantha. I'm glad my little smart-mouth, ungrateful, heifer is leaving for college. Now we can have a life, too!"

LILLY: "And, I just might dye my hair."

(The stage lights dim to black)

SCENE 2

(Sarah is in her bedroom, sitting in her rocking chair. Lilly gives her a cup of coffee as Iris looks on. Sarah takes the cup and begins to sip.)

LILLY: "You know, Mama… the only reason I've continued to keep *Cleo's Place* open, and in the family, is because one day it may be safe for Cleo to return home… Then the place would be waiting for him. **(Pause)** But it's been years… and I'm afraid Cleo is dead."

SARAH: "You may have given up, **(Pause)** but I won't… until the day I die!"

LILLY: (Almost in tears) "I'm sorry for what I said, Mama… I still have hope, too."

SARAH: "I know you love your brother. **(Pause)** If Cleo could send you a message right now… he would tell you to do what you think is best."

IRIS: "Lilly… what are your plans?"

LILLY: "With the money we have saved and the land you inherited—we can build us a new home and still have some money to live on!" **(Pause)** What do y'all think about that idea?"

IRIS: "Sounds good to me."

LILLY: "What about you, Mama."

SARAH: "I agree… ONLY if I can share in the expenses."

LILLY: "Mama, you don't have any money."

SARAH: "I'm going to make you eat your words."

(Sarah stands up and walks over to her bed and removes a dingy pillowcase from between her mattresses.)

IRIS: "Mama, what are you doing?"

SARAH: (Boastfully) "Preparing to make your mama eat her words… **(Pause)** Lilly… untie this bag and dump the stuff out on my mattress."

(Lilly unties the pillowcase and dumps its contents. Twenty thousand dollars tumble out of the pillowcase. Lilly and Iris scream with joy.)

IRIS: "Look at all of this MONEY!"

SARAH: "Lilly, I want you and Iris to take this money and build us the BEST DAMN COLORED-FOLKS HOME in Cross Town, Georgia."

IRIS: "Thank you, Mama… Thank YOU!"

LILLY: "Mama… where in the HELL did you get all of this MONEY?"

SARAH: "I'm only going to tell you once… So you better listen."

(Lilly and Iris sit on the mattress next to Sarah and the money.)

LILLY: "We're listening, Mama… Tell us!"

SARAH: "Iris, do you remember the day you went to work with me and I found Parker James dead in his bed?"

IRIS: "I don't think I'll ever forget that day… It was the first time I ever saw a dead person."

SARAH: "Remember the letter Mr. James left on his bedroom table for Dr. Baxter... and we read it?"

IRIS: "I certainly do!"

SARAH: "Tell Lilly what Parker James wrote in that letter."

IRIS: (Trying to remember) "Let me think… It went something like… 'The house Sarah lives in, I give to her. The three hundred dollars I left under my pillow is for Dr. Baxter to bury me. My store, I leave to Cross Town, Georgia… and whoever wants my fortune… will have to find it.' **(Pause)** Is that about right, Mama?"

SARAH: "You forgot he left me his mule, Sue, who I sold to my good friend, Wade… but you remembered close enough. **(Laughing)** Girls you're looking at the person who found Parker James' fortune."

LILLY: (Surprised) "Mama? Was Mr. James just teasing and had already given you his money?"

SARAH: "He should've, but he didn't. **(Pause)** After all those years that I worked for that man, being a slave to his every wish—I wasn't good enough for him to leave me his money. **(Angry)** He just left me this ratty house and a mule!"

IRIS: "Mama, how did you know where to look?"

SARAH: "I'm going to tell you. **(Pausing for a second)** One morning, Parker James got very angry at me because I didn't make him a fresh batch of biscuits. He said, **(Mocking)** 'That's why I'm not going to leave you any of my money! Before I do, I'll take it to my grave!' **(Pause)** I may not be educated, but I'm not stupid. **(Pause)** That's when I got my clue. **(Pause)** Iris, do you remember seeing that casket he kept in the corner of his room?"

IRIS: "I remember… It was so creepy!"

SARAH: "James kept that casket in his room so when he died it would be ready for his burial. **(Pause)** Anyway… if he said he was going to take his money with him to his grave… I figured it must be hidden in that casket… and I was right. **(Pause)** One day, I gave Parker James just a little more cough syrup than Dr. Baxter had prescribed… and when he was sound asleep, I carefully pulled up the padding in the bottom of that casket… and there it was… twenty thousand dollars… in twenties, fifties, and hundred-dollar bills. **(Pause)** You don't have to count it… I already have. **(Pause)** It's twenty thousand dollars."

LILLY: "That's a lot of money. **(Looking at the money laying on the mattress)** Mama, are you sure it's TWENTY THOUSAND DOLLARS?"

SARAH: "I can count. **(Pause)** If you don't believe me… count it for yourself."

IRIS: "Mama, I believe you. **(Pause)** You were the one who taught me how to count."

LILLY: "Did you take the money the day you found it?"

SARAH: "Not then. **(Pause)** I placed the padding back like it was over the money… just in case Parker James would check to see if it was still there. **(Pause)** I decided to wait until I found him dead and then I'd remove the money."

IRIS: "But, what would you have done if you weren't the one to find him dead?"

SARAH: (Forcefully and positive) "Oh… I was going to be the one. **(Pause)** I made sure I was going to be the one. **(Pause)** When I found him dead, I removed the money and stuffed it into that old pillowcase and fixed the coffin back neatly. **(Pause)** Then I hurried home with the money and hid it in Cleo's tool chest until I had time to put it under my mattress. **(Pause)** I ran back to town… went to Dr. Baxter's office and told him that I had found Mr. Parker James dead. **(Pause)** Those stupid white hicks destroyed every inch of that store… plank by plank… wasting their time… looking for that money!"

LILLY: (Looking at the money) "Mama… you deserve every penny of this money!"

SARAH: "I know I do. **(Pause)** With this money and the money Cleo left me plus the earnings from the café… we can begin building our new home on the land that Belinda left Iris and Samantha. **(Pause)** Maybe the house will be ready by spring when Samantha comes home to visit!"

LILLY: "What a great idea… But, where do we start?"

SARAH: "We'll start with *Conrad Davis & Son Construction Company*. They were the ones contracted to build that new school for the white children. My friend, Tom Willis, occasionally works for Mr. Davis and his crew. Tom says when it comes to construction… they are the best."

LILLY: "Yeah, Mama… they may be the best… but, when it comes to Mr. Conrad doing business with poor colored folks… he is a known crook that can't be trusted. **(Pause)** He has a way of stealing their farmland by convincing them to let his construction company build them a house… on their land… and he finances it. **(Pause)** When they miss one payment on their mortgage, he takes their house and land and sells it to some rich white people."

SARAH: "I know Conrad is a crook. **(Pause)** Tom has told me how he has robbed a lot of colored folks out of their land. **(Pause)** But, that won't happen to us! **(Pause)** We won't be like those other poor souls who forgot about the dry season… when the weather was too hot and dry… or too cold and rainy for their crops to yield enough profit to survive… much less, enough money to pay a mortgage. **(Pause)** We've got an advantage over them. We have enough money to pay cash for our house. **(Pause)** But… we must keep this a secret for now! **(Pause)** When we get an appointment to see Mr. Conrad… we must give him the impression that we're just some DUMB niggers, who were fortunate enough to inherit the land—the same land he already tried to buy from Mr. Henry's brother, Jim Boggs… and that we're just another colored family that he can scam."

LILLY: "Iris, help Mama put the money back under her mattress. **(Pause)** I'm going to go in the kitchen and cook us a big breakfast of fried ham, scrambled eggs, grits and BISCUITS!"

SARAH: (Laughing) "Make sure your biscuits are freshly made…. **(Reflecting on why Mr. Parker James didn't leave her his money)** I might get mad… and not leave you any of this twenty-thousand dollars."

(The stage lights dim to black)

SCENE 3

(It is the last day that Sarah, Lilly, and Iris will spend in their old house—the place they have called home for all these years. Sarah and Lilly are rummaging through their belongings, deciding what they will take to their newly built house or what they will leave behind. Iris stares out the kitchen window, wondering where all the years have gone.)

LILLY: (Laughing)

SARAH: "What's so funny?"

LILLY: "I was just thinking about the first day we walked into Mr. Conrad's office. It seems just like yesterday when that stupid son of his - wearing those tight khaki pants stuck in the crack of his big ass - invited us into his daddy's office. **(Mocking)** 'Daddy those three colored women, who want us to build them a house, is here.'"

SARAH: "His fat daddy was sitting behind his desk with his feet up and smoking a stinking cigar. **(Pause)** He didn't even stand to greet us. **(Pause)** He just sat there… with that sly smile on his face. **(Pause)** When we said we wanted him to build us a home and told him how large we wanted it… the first thing out of his mouth was asking us how could we afford such a luxury home. **(Pause)** He said even rich white people couldn't afford that kind of house… and he asked how we would pay for it."

LILLY: "You told him that we were owners of *Cleo's Place* **(Pause)** and your granddaughter and great-granddaughter had inherited all of Mr. Henry and Mrs. Emma Boggs' land. **(Pause)** That got his attention. **(Pause)** We had something he had always wanted… and that was all the land of Henry and Emma Boggs. **(Pause)** Now that some niggers owned it, he wasn't going to let that happen. **(Pause)** Right then, I knew he was going to build our house and begin plotting on how he was going to take it from us. **(Pause)** I must say… he did his best. **(Pause)** But, we were one step ahead of him. **(Pause)** After *Cleo's Place* burned to the ground… he thought we wouldn't be able to make our payment. Not only did we make the payments… but, we had enough money to pay it off in full."

SARAH: "*Cleo's Place* didn't just burn down… someone deliberately set it on fire. **(Pause)** I bet it was Conrad and them."

LILLY: "Remember, Mama… Mr. Conrad sent Mr. Jack Jones over to our house for him to tell you that he wanted to see us at the court house in Judge Crews' office."

SARAH: "It was the next day after *Cleo's Place* had burned down. **(Pause)** That crook, Mr. Conrad, wasn't even decent enough to wait and give us one day to get over our shock. **(Pause)** When we arrived at the courthouse, he and Judge Crews were already waiting for us. **(Pause)** But when he left that courthouse, he left with his ass tucked between his legs **(Pause)** and we left there owning our home, fully paid off."

(Sarah and Lilly begin to laugh.)

LILLY: "Mama, are you going to miss this old house?"

SARAH: (Sarcastically angry) "Miss it? Nah… I won't miss it… neither will I miss the rats playing in the attic; using a chamber pot for a toilet; cooking on a wood burning stove; washing clothes and taking a bath in a bucket; rainwater dripping through the ceiling; nor us freezing our asses off trying to keep warm by the fireplace."

LILLY: (Relieved) "Well… we won't have any of those problems at our new house. **(Pause)** We'll have our own bedroom… with new beds and mattresses… and an inside bathroom with a tub… and hot running water."

SARAH: "Don't forget we'll have the choice of eating in the kitchen or in the dining room… lounging in the living room or sitting in the swing on the porch. **(Pause)** But… even with all the miserable years we spent in this old house… there were a few good memories. **(Pause)** John, Cleo, you, and Rose were born right here in this house. **(Pause)** I nursed and rocked all four of you, to sleep, in this here old, rocking chair. **(Touching the rocking chair)** Y'all would be playing and sitting under the chinaberry tree… waiting for me when I got home from work. **(Regretfully)** I wish I had been more tolerant with John, Cleo, and Rose… I know John's dead. **(Pause)** Rose and Cleo… **(Doubtful)** I just don't know. **(Pause)** Lilly…

LILLY: "Yes, Mama."

SARAH: "Do you think I'll ever see Rose and Cleo before I die?"

LILLY: "I promise, Mama… **(Stuttering)** I… I… I truly believe you will!"

SARAH: "Lilly… You've been a good daughter to me."

LILLY: "Thank you, Mama."

SARAH: (Changing the subject) "Now that I got that said… What keepsakes are you taking with you?"

LILLY: "Besides our family album and the Bible with our birthdates recorded inside… I don't want anything else. **(Pause)** I'm leaving everything behind… even my old clothes and shoes. **(Pause)** What are you taking?"

SARAH: (Removing a framed picture of a young soldier hanging on the wall) "I'm leaving everything… except John's picture, my rocking chair, and wash pots. **(Pause)** I wish I could find my white, lace handkerchief John gave me. It just disappeared. **(Sadly)** It meant so much to me."

LILLY: (Noticing that Iris is disengaged and looking out the window) "Iris… this will be our last day in this old house before it's torn down. **(Pause)** If you have anything you want to take with you… this is your last chance."

IRIS: "There's nothing I want."

LILLY: (Concerned) "You've been looking out that window for a very long time… What's on your mind? **(Pause)** Share your thoughts with Mama and me."

IRIS: (Reflecting) "I was just looking at that old chinaberry tree and all those ripe berries that have fallen on the ground… and remembering me hiding behind it when Mama was going to give me a whipping. **(Pause)** I'm looking at the peach trees Mama planted… and remembering the sweet smells of the blossoms on those long hot summer evenings… and the taste of the pies Mama made from the wormy peaches. **(Pause)** I remember helping Mama plant her vegetable and flower gardens… and scrubbing clothes and bathing in buckets… and all those boarders that once lived in this house. **(Silence for a second)** Mama… I heard you asking Lilly would you ever see Cleo or Rose again… and it made me think. **(Hopelessly sad)** Will I ever see my only child, Samantha, again?"

LILLY: "You will, Iris… I promise you will."

IRIS: "I don't know Lilly. All I get are letters from Samantha. **(Pause)** Now she has left college, gotten married, and moved to California. **(Pause)** We don't know anything about the man she married. I hope he's good to her and she's happy."

LILLY: "Iris… when we get settled in the new house… you should go and visit Samantha and ask her why she's *breaking the chain* with her family."

SARAH: "Iris, please don't make the same mistakes I made with Rose. **(Regretful)** If I could go back to that day… I would do things differently. **(Pause)** If I had accepted Charlie Sweet into our family… I would still have my Rose, grandchild, and maybe some more grandchildren. **(Pause)** Because of my selfish reasoning… I don't know where my youngest daughter is. **(Pause)** Go to Samantha… Tell her that we love her… and we want her to come home."

IRIS: (Turning away from the window and facing Sarah) "Mama… that's exactly what I'm going to do. **(Pause)** As soon as we get settled in the new house… I'm going to fly to California and visit her. **(Pause)** We're going to have a long needed mother-daughter talk. **(Looking at Lilly)** Lilly… do you want to come with me? **(Pause)** It will be our first time on an airplane."

LILLY: "I'll have to think about it. **(Pause)** You know I'm scared of flying."

IRIS: (Looking at Sarah) "Mama… what about you? Will you go with us? **(Pause)** I'm sure Samantha would love to see you."

SARAH: "You and Lilly can go without me. **(Looking into the distance)** Something tells me… I won't be up to it by then."

IRIS: "What do you mean, Mama?"

SARAH: (About to answer Iris, but is interrupted by Lilly.)

LILLY: (Reaching in a pasteboard box filled with junk and finding Miss Ann, Iris' old doll) "Iris… isn't this the doll I gave you years ago?"

IRIS: (Shocked and almost childlike) "Miss Ann! **(Quickly taking Miss Ann from Lilly, with the same joy as the first day she received her years ago)** I thought I'd never see you again! **(Pause)** Now I can leave this house in peace! **(Pause)** Mama and Lilly… I found what I'm taking to our new home… My beloved Miss Ann. **(Looking into the face**

of the small doll) Miss Ann… you're coming home with me.

(Iris is still embracing her moment of joy. Sarah reaches for Lilly's hand and they briefly hold hands before walking over to Iris. Sarah and Lilly are now standing next to Iris, silently celebrating with her. Sarah and Lilly then put their arms around Iris, each hugging her from the side with one arm on her waist. Miss Ann is still in Iris' hand.)

(The stage lights dim to black)

SCENE 4

(Lilly and Iris are in the living room of their new home. They are sitting at opposite ends of the couch. Lilly is to the far right and Iris is to the far left of the couch, with an empty space between them. Their furnishings are modest, but an upgrade from their last house. On the wall hang three framed pictures, one trimmed in gold and two in wood. In the gold frame is a picture of Sarah with gray hair. In one of the wooden frames is a picture of a middle-aged Lilly and in the other wooden frame is a picture of a young Samantha. Sarah's old rocking chair sits near the pictures.)

LILLY: "I can't believe it's been almost two years since Mama died. **(Pause)** She was always the first to get up and have breakfast cooking on the stove. **(Pause)** When I didn't smell her buttery biscuits, fried ham, scrambled eggs with cheese, and grits—I knew something was wrong. **(Pause)** I hate that Mama didn't get to enjoy our new home. I'm so sad that she died within the first month of us moving here."

IRIS: "Mama was still in bed when I went to check on her. **(Pause)** She was lying on her back and her eyes were fixed on the ceiling. **(Pause)** I thought she was dead until she tried to speak. **(Pause)** I couldn't understand a word she was saying. **(Pause)** That's when I screamed for you."

LILLY: "I didn't know what Mama was trying to say either… until I put my ear very close to her mouth. **(Pause)** Mama told me that she was dying. **(Pause)** I told her to hold on and that I was going to send you to get the doctor. **(Pause)** I remember her whispering, 'No.' **(Pause)** She just wanted me to sit and hold her hand until the end. **(Standing up from the couch)** Mama's prediction was right. **(Pause)** Just a week earlier… when we were down at the creek fishing… she told me that her time left on this earth was near because she felt cold chills running deep into her bones. **(Pause)** It was strange because it was a hot day. **(Pause)** She told me that she wanted a graveside burial and to bury her in her pink dress and white gloves. **(Pause)** She wanted Reverend Wade Crowder to recite the *Twenty-Third Psalm* and for Miss Carrie Williams to sing *Amazing Grace.* **(Looking at and slightly touching the framed picture of Sarah)** Mama didn't ask for much… so I was determined that she got her last wish… and she did!"

IRIS: "I thought we wouldn't ever find Reverend Crowder's house… but you kept driving down those winding dirt roads… far into the backwoods. **(Pause)** I kept telling you that no human could live down here… but you kept saying, 'Oh yes there could.' You kept repeating, 'I remember visiting him with Mama when I was a little girl.' **(Pause)** You didn't give up either… until you found his house."

LILLY: (Laughing) "I sure didn't! **(Pause)** Mama was going to get her wish even if it was the last thing I ever did."

IRIS: "I couldn't believe my eyes when I saw the Crowder's old house, covered with kudzu vines and the roof caving in on one side. **(Pause)** It was shabbier than the house we use to live in! **(Pause)** I guess he and his wife, Louise, had just been forgotten… like their abandoned cotton fields and their empty pasture that their old mule, Sue, who Mama sold to him for ten dollars… those many years ago… once grazed. **(Pause)** When Rev. Crowder came to the door and you told him who we were, he was so happy to see us. **(Pause)** I can still remember the look on his face when he greeted us."

LILLY: (Sitting back down on the couch) And GIRL did he preach a good sermon that day! **(Pause)** And I've never heard anyone sing **(Singing the words)** '*Amazing Grace how sweet the sound that saved a wretch like me*' as beautiful as Miss Carrie Williams did.

IRIS: (Turning to look at the picture frame of Sarah as she continues to sit on the couch) Rest in peace Mama. **(Reminiscing and laughing)** I've never met anyone like my grandma Sarah."

LILLY: (Laughing) "My mama was one of a kind. **(Pause)** She either loved you or hated you. There was no in-between. **(Sarcastically)**

I will never forget that last day in our old house when she thanked me for being a good daughter and told me she loved me. **(More serious)** It set my heart FREE!"

IRIS: "Mama and I got very close before she died. We talked about a lot of things… But she wouldn't tell me anything about my daddy. **(Pause)** When I would bring up the subject, she would say, 'Ask Lilly. She's the one to tell you.' **(Silence)** Lilly, now that we're both old adults… don't you think it's time I knew something about the man who was my father? **(Pause)** Aunt Rose told me his name was George Dawson. **(Pause)** When he got you pregnant, he skipped town with the help of Mrs. Cora Mae and that was why Mama hated her."

LILLY: "I guess everyone wants to know something about their daddy. **(Pause)** Even at my age, I wish I would've had the courage to ask Mama more about Mr. Parker James—the white man who treated her like a slave and fathered me, John, Cleo, and Rose. **(Pause)** Now it's too late. **(Pause)** But, it's not too late for you. **(Pause)** Iris, I'm going to tell you about your father… but it's not a pretty story. **(Pause)** Your father's name was George Dawson; He came to Cross Town looking for Mr. Parker James to do some business. From my understanding, Mr. Parker James use to find him construction jobs building schools and other things around town. Mr. James asked Mama would she board him in our house… and she agreed. **(Pause)** He looked white, but Mama said he was colored. **(Pause)** He lived with us and began to date Mama. **(Pause)** When Mama went to work and left us alone with George… he would send Cleo hunting and Rose outdoors to play. **(Pause)** Then he would take me to his room and rape me. **(Realizing what was done to her)** Iris… I was just a child… I didn't know what I was doing. **(Angrily)** He was so mean to us when Mama wasn't around! **(Pause)** He use to tell me that I was evil… and if I ever told Mama what he was doing… that he would take me into the woods and bury me alive. **(Pause)** He would always remind me that Mama would never find my body."

IRIS: "How did Mama find out what George was doing to you?"

LILLY: "One day, Rose found the courage to tell."

IRIS: "What did Mama do?"

LILLY: "Mama would have killed George if she could've found him. **(Standing up from the couch and prancing intermittingly)** Mrs. Cora Mae hid him at her house until she and George could catch a midnight train out of Georgia. **(Laughing)** But George skipped out on Mrs. Cora Mae, too."

IRIS: "I bet he never showed his face in Cross Town again."

LILLY: "Oh, yes he DID! He had the nerve to come by the house when you were four years old."

IRIS: (Shocked) "Did he see me?"

LILLY: "No... You were in the house asleep. **(Pause)** Mama and I were cleaning catfish in the backyard. **(Pause)** George just walked right up to us. **(Pause)** Mama recognized him right away, but I didn't until she said **(Mimicking)** 'George Dawson... what in the hell is you doing here?' **(Pause)** He said 'I'm here to see my daughter, Iris.' **(Pause)** He no longer looked like the big, tall, handsome man he once did when he fled Cross Town like a sneaky rat in the night. **(Pause)** He looked like he was knocking on hell's door... He was skinny, slumped over, and sickly."

IRIS: "How did he know I was a girl... and what my name was?"

LILLY: "Mr. Parker James knew where he was and probably told him."

IRIS: "Did you or Mama let him see me?"

LILLY: "Mama was holding the bloody butcher knife that she was using to clean catfish. **(Gesturing with her hands like Sarah had)** She held it up and pointed it directly at George. **(Pause)** She told him, **(Mimicking)** 'You'll see the bowels of Hell before you see my grandchild... Get the hell out of my yard before I gut you like a fish!'"

IRIS: "Did he leave?"

LILLY: (Sitting back down on the couch) "Right then… He could barely keep his footing as he walked down the road towards town. **(Pause)** That was the last time that we ever saw or heard from George. **(Pause)** Three weeks later, Mr. Parker James told Mama that George died as soon as he made it back to Texas. **(Silence)** I'm sorry Iris… but I don't have anything kind to say about your daddy! He was not a good man. **(Reaching across the empty seat with her right hand and grabbing Iris' left hand)** I love you, and Mama loved you. **(Pause)** I have never regretted having you as my daughter."

IRIS: "I understand… and I always knew you loved me. **(Putting her right hand on top of Lilly's right hand, which still grasps her left hand.)** One of these days I'll tell you about what happened to me a long time ago."

LILLY: "Does it have something to do with Mama's old boarder, Mr. Joe Fish?"

IRIS: (Pulling her hands quickly back, causing Lilly to also let go of her hand.) "How did you know?"

LILLY: "I just knew. **(Pause)** Iris… let it go. **(Pause)** It wasn't your fault. **(Pause)** George is dead… and I'm sure Mr. Fish is probably dead too. **(Recognizing the childlike and stunned expression on Iris' face)** You and Miss Ann are safe now. **(Standing up from the couch)** From this day forward…let us put our bad memories behind us."

IRIS: (Also standing up) "Thank you, Lilly, for telling me all of this. **(Pause)** I feel like a heavy load has been lifted off my soul. **(Pause)** Tomorrow is Thanksgiving. Let's go to the store, buy a fat turkey, and cook a big dinner just for you and me. **(Walking over and putting her hand on Lilly's shoulder)** We can stay up and cook all night!"

LILLY: "Well… Let's get started!" **(They walk of stage together as the stage lights dim to black.)**

SCENE 5

(This scene reverts back to an older Iris who is in her living room with the mailman, Mr. Cooper. It continues where SCENE 1 **ended. Iris is rocking back and forth in Sarah's old rocking chair, clutching a white handkerchief in her hand. She has just finished telling Mr. Cooper her story.)**

IRIS: "Mr. Cooper… after my dear mother, Lilly, opened up to me about her troubled past… we became closer than I could've ever imagined. **(Pause)** I found myself admiring and loving her for those few wonderful years we had together before she died peacefully in her sleep. **(A few seconds of silence passes before Iris again speaks)**… And that's my story… from start to finish."

MR. COOPER: "Wow… what an interesting life you've had. **(Pause)** Miss Iris… Do you have any relatives left in Cross Town?"

IRIS: "No… I'm afraid I don't. **(Pause)** I never saw or heard from my Aunt Rose or Uncle Cleo again. **(Pause)** I assume they're probably dead by now. **(Pause)** The only relatives I have left are my daughter Samantha, who never comes to visit me, and her two children, that I've never seen."

MR. COOPER: "I know all too well, Miss Iris. **(Pause)** I'm in a similar situation myself. **(Standing up from the couch)** I guess I better get going before it gets too late. **(Grabbing his mailbag before building up the courage to ask a question)** Miss Iris… if it's all right with you… can I drop by and visit sometimes after I finish my mail route? **(Pause)** You know… just to sit and talk."

IRIS: (slightly smiling and blushing) "Mr. Cooper… it would be my pleasure."

MR. COOPER: "What about tomorrow?"

IRIS: "Tomorrow will be fine."

MR. COOPER: (Walking closer towards the door) "Enjoy the rest of your day, Miss Iris."

IRIS: (Following him to the door) "You too. **(Pause)** See you tomorrow, Mr. Cooper?"

MR. COOPER: "That's a promise."

(Mr. Cooper exits the stage. Iris stands in the doorway waving as he walks away. She shakes her head then turns to go back towards Sarah's rocking chair, with a nostalgic smile on her face. Iris stands for a moment before picking up her old letters in one hand while clutching a white handkerchief in the other. She sits in Sarah's old rocking chair

as the stage lights are now focused just on her, with everything else in darkness. She looks down at the letters and pauses before bringing the handkerchief up to one eye as though to wipe away tears.)

IRIS: "Promises, Promises, Promises."

(The stage lights dim to black)

THE END

We hope you enjoyed reading *Broken Promises*….

Turn the page to learn how to contact us and view Wise Scholars Publishing's other literary selections.

Available in Paperback, Hardback, & E-Book

Available in Paperback, Hardback, & E-Book

CONTACT US

www.wisescholarspublishing.com

www.facebook.com/wisescholarspublishing

wisescholarspublishing

@marshalettewise

marshalette@wisescholarspublishing.com

1-888-735-6392

1-334-452-4596 (Fax)

www.ingramcontent.com/pod-product-compliance
Lightning Source LLC
Chambersburg PA
CBHW081135300726
48982CB00005B/972

* 9 7 8 0 9 9 6 3 9 4 6 6 6 *